"I love you," Lauren whispered in Aimee's ear.

Aimee pulled away and looked at her, "Then show me."

Lauren lead her upstairs.

"All I ever wanted was you."

Aimee kissed her.

Lauren slowly took off Aimee's shirt, watching her. Aimee quivered as Lauren kissed her breasts. Lauren undressed her and pushed her gently toward the bed.

"You are so beautiful," Lauren said, kissing her neck. "I've wanted to touch you from the moment I met you."

"But it's not polite to grope a stranger," Aimee teased, pulling Lauren's clothes off.

Visit

Bella Books

at

BellaBooks.com

or call our toll-free number

1-800-729-4992

SWEET FIRE

BY
SAXON BENNETT

Bella
BOOKS

2000

Bella Books, Inc.
P.O. Box 10543
Tallahassee, FL 32302

Printed in the United States of America on acid-free paper
First Edition, Second Printing

Editor: Lila Empson
Cover designer: Bonnie Liss (Phoenix Graphics)

ISBN 0-9677753-5-3

To Lulu R.
for wondering if she is in this book

And to answer your question,
yes, Lulu, you fill every book with
a little bit of Lulu wisdom.

About the Author

Saxon Bennett is currently in transition. She is seeking a change of locale and a new outlook; perhaps it is a midlife crisis, the climate, pollution, and overpopulation that are causing this. Aren't novels born of just this kind of stuff? She does have two new furry family members, Sarah and Gunther, who supply big moments of gleeful distraction.

One

Aimee Nishimo stood with her lover, Pamela, in downtown Heroy, New Mexico, looking up at the signboard overhead: HOPE'S UNIVERSE, AN ALTERNATIVE BOOKSTORE.

"She did it. She made her dream come true," Pamela said.

"She dreamt of a bookstore?" Aimee queried.

"One just like this. We used to talk about it."

"I thought you wanted her to be an associate professor," Aimee said.

"Things were different back then," Pamela replied.

Five years had passed since Pamela had seen Hope. They had kept in touch much to Aimee's chagrin, especially in those early days when their love affair should have been blossoming into those gilded moments of memory that sustain every relationship when things get rough. Aimee finally got Pamela to admit it was strange to be looking for solace with the woman who broke her heart, but somehow it had worked. Calling Hope always put Pamela in a better mood and made her a more cordial lover, and for that Aimee was prepared to despise the woman who still held her lover's heart.

The wick was ignited in this Molotov cocktail of a relationship when Pamela told Aimee of the research project she had planned for the summer. Pamela assumed Aimee would come along because the book project required the two of them.

And now they were standing in front of Pamela's ex-lover's bookstore in a small town in the middle of nowhere. A town purported to contain more lesbians per capita than any other place on the planet. Aimee begged to differ on this point, suggesting that New York, Minneapolis, and San Francisco touted more dykes then Heroy. But Pamela insisted those cities did not boast such a close-knit community. Pamela and Aimee were about to embark on a study of lesbian community life, write a book about it, and get the rest of a rather large advance. This would have been exciting if Hope Kaznot hadn't lived in Heroy.

The door to the shop swung open as a customer left, and Aimee felt foolish standing there like a country bumpkin who'd never seen a gay bookstore before.

"Maybe we should call first?" Aimee suggested, getting cold feet.

"It'll be all right. It might even be fun," Pamela said, tucking her dark braid back and straightening her shoulders.

She postures like that when she's nervous, Aimee thought. Being a student of human interrelations, she had made her girlfriend a primary study. Using the word *fun* meant there could potentially be a disastrous edge. Aimee smiled facetiously and held the door open.

The blond woman behind the counter looked up. She was an attractive woman, but she was hardly the stunning

2

creature Aimee had concocted in her head of Pamela's love of a lifetime. Aimee nodded politely. Pamela smiled at her as well and went about fingering the selection of postcards on the counter. Aimee followed her lead and went to the magazine rack, glad for this moment's reprieve. Facing her nemesis made Aimee's heart quicken a beat and gave her an adrenaline rush. Aimee dreaded times like these. She was on the verge of telling Pamela that maybe she should meet Hope alone when another blond woman came in from the back room.

"Crystal, I found it. I knew we had it. What sort of a bookstore would we be if we didn't? Damn, I've got to figure out a better way to organize the antiquities section," the woman said, balancing the book on her head and doing a three-quarter French turn. She looked like a model, Aimee thought. *This* woman was very pretty. The woman's face went from pleased to mortified in a matter of seconds. Pamela does seem to have that effect on people, Aimee mused to herself.

"Pamela?" The book dropped and landed on top of Hope's sandal. Mortified moved to pained. Another Pamela effect, Aimee thought. Hope sunk to the ground and grabbed her foot.

"Are you all right? It's not broken is it?" Crystal asked, coming to her boss's side. "Let me see."

"What are you doing here?" Hope said, looking up from her crippled appendage.

"A research project on lesbian community life. I thought Heroy would be the perfect place."

Crystal scurried for some ice.

"That's the problem with old books; they're awfully heavy," Crystal said, picking up the book. "For shit's sake, it must weigh ten pounds. Are you sure it's not broken?"

"I think it's just a bruise," Hope said.

They all peered at it.

"It's not pretty," Aimee said.

"No," Hope replied looking up at Aimee.

3

"Where are my manners? I should introduce you two. Aimee Nishimo meet Hope Kaznot," Pamela said, giving Hope a hand up. Hope limped to the counter and eased up on a stool.

"Nice to finally meet you. I've heard so much about you," Hope said.

"And you, too," Aimee replied, thinking to herself that Hope was beautiful, gorgeous in fact, and she's probably really nice and has an incredible partner and a perfect life.

"Don't I even get a hug?" Pamela asked.

Hope held out her arms, "I'm not standing on this foot until the throbbing stops."

"Perfectly understandable," Pamela said.

"You shouldn't surprise someone like that," Hope said, holding her.

"I thought it would be fun," Pamela replied, closing her eyes and pulling Hope tight.

There's that operative word again, *fun*, Aimee thought. Impending disaster. Ex-wife is gorgeous and still pulls on the heart strings. Beware: Summer from hell ahead, she warned herself. She should have stayed in New York. Maybe absence would have made Pamela's heart grow fonder. Aimee hadn't quite figured out what was going wrong in their relationship, but something was and it was going wrong quickly. Aimee tried to imagine Pamela and Hope together. Nice looking couple, but Hope seemed too down to earth for Pamela's taste.

Hope repositioned the ice back on her foot. "So you're doing a research project. It sounds interesting. Interviewing the town lesbians?"

"Yes. I was kind of hoping you could get us started by introducing us and convincing potential participants."

"Of course. We'll get Berlin going, and she'll have half the town beating down your door to tell you their story. How long are you staying?" Hope inquired.

"Actually, the summer. We're writing a book, so I thought we'd start and get at least a rough draft before we left. That

4

way, if there's holes we can fill them in while we still have access to the surroundings."

"The entire summer?" Hope asked.

"Yes, we'll rent a place," Pamela replied.

The courthouse chimes rang out one o'clock.

"Why, yes, of course, rent a place," Hope said, "I think the O'Malley place is still looking to lease until they find a buyer. It's a nice house."

Hope got down abruptly and limped toward the front door. "Perhaps we should go get something cold to drink, talk to Berlin, and get things started.

"All right, I'd like a tour of the store, though," Pamela said.

"We have all summer for that," Hope said, looking over at Crystal. "Maybe you should go and find Emerson."

"Why? She'll be back any time," Crystal replied cheerfully.

"Exactly. You go and find her." Hope said, throwing her a meaningful glance. "I'll give Pamela and Aimee the tour of the store, and then we'll go have drinks," Hope said, pulling them in the opposite direction.

She's hiding something, Aimee deduced smugly.

"Okay, I'll be right back then," Crystal said.

But it was too late, Emerson came sauntering in the back door with a little girl riding high on the shoulders.

"Shit!" Hope said, grimacing.

"Mama, mama, ecoutez, au jour d'hui, j'apprend du *Le Petit Prince*."

Emerson swung her off her shoulders and toward Hope. The little girl wrapped her legs around Hope's waist, smiled prettily, and kissed her mother.

"Trés bien ma petite anana. Je t'aime. Tu es trés faime?"

"Oui, je voudrais deux sandwiches au jambon avec les pomme frites et beaucoup patisseries."

Emerson and Hope both laughed. Aimee was frantically trying to recall her freshman French class. It was something about a ham sandwich.

Pamela stood stunned.

"I'm sorry. I meant to tell you . . . I just never knew quite how," Hope fumbled.

Emerson looked at both Pamela and Aimee. "Pamela?"

"Hello, Emerson. This is my partner, Aimee," Pamela said, trying to recover her composure.

"Nice to meet you," Emerson said, extending a hand.

"And this little monster is Nicole," Hope said, swinging her down. "These are my friends Pamela and Aimee. Say hello, little one."

Nicole stuck out her tiny little hand to shake. "Nice to meet you," she said politely.

Aimee smiled with relief. She was beginning to think Nicole didn't speak English. Hope seemed to read her mind.

"We have a very nice older woman who came from Paris to live with her daughter. She's teaching the children French. It makes her happy."

"All right you two, I'm off," Emerson said.

"Time to meet the Dragon Lady," Nicole chanted.

"You be good," Emerson said, kissing the top of Nicole's head.

Emerson kissed Hope's cheek, "I'll see you later. Lauren just wants to go over the details before we ship off the sculptures."

"Mama and I are going to be famous. Emerson made us pretty in stone and is sending us to a big museum in New York," Nicole told them.

And then it dawned on Aimee. She kept looking at Hope and couldn't figure out why she seemed familiar. She had been the model for the beautiful bronze piece in Pamela's apartment. A cold knot of anger formed inside Aimee's chest. Pamela lied. Aimee felt someone take her hand. She looked down and saw Nicole.

"I really like your hair."

"Probably cause it looks a lot like yours," Aimee said. They both had short, spiky hair.

"I used to have long hair, but I didn't like anyone to comb it. So one day I cut it all off by myself," Nicole said.

"Yes, she did," Hope said.

"Did you have long hair before?" Nicole asked.

"I did," Aimee said. "And then one day I cut it all off too."

"Because you didn't want anyone to comb it?"

"No, because I needed a change," Aimee said.

"She wanted a new life," Pamela added.

"Do you like ice cream?" Nicole asked.

"I love ice cream," Aimee said.

"Want to go get some with me? We could talk."

"How old are you?" Aimee asked, catching Pamela's eye.

"Five, almost six, I'm just small for my age."

"I think you've made a friend," Pamela said.

"Is that all right with you?" Aimee asked Hope.

"Sure. You can treat Aimee. Tell Berlin to put it on your account."

"Yeah!"

"Shall we go get a cold one?" Hope asked Pamela.

"Please."

Pamela looked at Aimee. "So I'll meet you back here?"

"If you'd like," Aimee said, her disdain more than evident.

"Why don't you two come for dinner at the house? I'll barbecue a salmon," Emerson said.

Hope smiled at her appreciatively.

"I'll bring you home," Nicole said.

"It'll be nice. Please come," Hope said.

7

"All right," Aimee said, trying to put her anger at Pamela away temporarily. They would talk later. It was awfully hard not to like Hope and her family, and suddenly Aimee didn't have the necessary will power. The summer loomed in front of her dismally. The sooner she got used to it and got back to work, the better off she'd be. Maybe her nemesis was really a guardian angel in disguise.

Aimee spent the afternoon in the café getting the history of everyone's relationships. Berlin Queen was one of Nic's extended family. She was married to Katherine Du Pont, who was Emerson's surrogate mother after her mother had died giving birth to her. Katherine had been in love with Emerson's mother before she got married, and she had gracefully bowed out when Emerson's father offered a well-established conventional lifestyle and a child. Katherine's daughter, Rachel, and Emerson had grown up together, and it was Rachel who had brought Hope out to Heroy that fateful summer when she fell in love with Emerson.

Berlin told the stories and Nic patiently listened as Aimee began to understand some of what this town was about. When they left the café with a warm hug from Berlin, Aimee felt better. At least if she was going to fall out of love, Heroy would be a much better place to be depressed in than New York. In Berlin, Aimee felt she had found a kindred spirit. Every place she had ever lived required such a spirit. What she lacked in family she made up for in friends. Right now Aimee needed a friend.

Pamela and Hope sat at the bar of Joe's Espresso and had Long Island iced teas. The sky was an incredible blue with no promise of a cloud, and the breeze blew Hope's peasant dress about her bare ankles.

"You look good. Different, but good. You look more —"

"Feminine?" Hope queried.

8

"Well, yes," Pamela replied.

"I can't help it. I just sort of got that way," Hope said, trying not to feel apologetic.

"There's nothing wrong with it," Pamela said, touching Hope's hand. "It suits you."

Their eyes met.

"Thank you," Hope said, embarrassed by the intimacy.

"Hope, why didn't you tell me about Nicole?"

"I didn't think you'd be interested."

"Hope —"

"I was afraid," Hope admitted, thinking of the times when she was pregnant and talking to Pamela on the phone. She should have told her, but she was afraid of the judgment Pamela would have inevitably made concerning her new life's course. Most of their long distance calls were consumed by Pamela's latest set of neuroses. That was easier to deal with than telling her ex-lover that she was madly in love with Emerson and that they were planning a family.

"Why?" Pamela asked, glaring.

"I was sure you'd think it was a betrayal of your feminist values. Motherhood and all," Hope replied, raising her eyebrows and taking a sip of her drink.

"I can't believe you'd underestimate me like that. My views on motherhood as an institution — which was historically used to enslave women and keep them tied to the hearth and thus unable to achieve their other potentials — has no bearing when it comes to lesbian motherhood as a choice. Having a child outside of patriarchy is not a betrayal of feminist values. If anything, you are reclaiming the institution and remaking it," Pamela said, her gray eyes flashing with an anger Hope was all too familiar with.

"I'm sorry. I didn't mean to hurt you," Hope said, doing her best to pacify Pamela. Hope felt her neck and shoulders tense up. She felt like she was in graduate school again, where Pamela's views were the only ones available.

"You did," Pamela said firmly.

"Aimee seems nice," Hope said, trying to change the subject.

"She is. I don't treat her as well as I should," Pamela said, twisting her signet ring.

"Pamela, what's wrong?" Hope asked, knowing that if she didn't push Pamela to the wall quickly they would never get to the bottom of this.

"Midlife crisis, perhaps," Pamela ventured.

"You really believe in that stuff?" Hope replied with a heretic's face.

"I don't know what it is. I just feel so lost sometimes, like I can't seem to find the things I need in order to feel good about my life."

"Is that why you're here?" Hope asked, secretly praying that her life was not somehow intertwined with Pamela's quest for personal nirvana. Hope didn't have the heart to tell Pamela that happiness is not a perpetual state of mind, that life comprises tedious, unpleasant, hectic, sad, and disappointing moments, which the heights of achievements cannot stave off. The quest was a moot point. But how does one tell an overachiever such a horrid thing? How does one bring the tent of illusion crashing down? Hope took a deep breath and tried to relax her shoulders and think good thoughts.

"Yes," Pamela replied.

"What do you expect to find?" Hope asked.

Pamela flagged the bartender.

"Is that a good idea?" Hope inquired.

"You're not cooking."

"No, I'm not," Hope said, slurping on her straw and smiling at Pamela.

The sky was turning pink across the mountains as Aimee, Emerson, and Nic sat at the picnic table in the backyard. They were playing Old Maid, Nic's favorite card game, rescued from Berlin and Katherine's attic where it had been carefully hid when Aunt Rachel was a child and Berlin refused to play one more hand. Nic found the cards and had been torturing the adults with her latest obsession. Berlin kept threatening to teach her poker if those infernal cards didn't go missing soon. Aimee was having her second beer and starting to feel the glow of benevolence that evening cocktails bring. Emerson didn't drink, so she was having a soda and Nic was sipping a Shirley Temple complete with umbrella. Berlin had taught Nic everything she knew about tending bar. Emerson didn't think it was such a good idea, but Berlin taught Nic things out of love.

"I mean, how can I refuse? Of course, the looming threat of a five-year-old card-shark bartender does have me more than a little concerned," Emerson explained.

Emerson was doing her best to be a good hostess. Hope had taught her a lot of things in the five years. She wanted to make Hope proud. She told Aimee about her work, about being a parent, about learning to be a good partner.

"I was not always this civilized," Emerson said, as she rolled the salmon into tinfoil, neatly folding the corners.

"So what *were* you like?" Aimee asked, smiling coyly at Emerson.

"Just this side of barbaric," Emerson said.

"Why were you so barbaric?" Aimee inquired.

"Because I thought people were assholes."

"And now they're not?" Aimee asked.

"Now I have more tolerance," Emerson replied with a definiteness that surprised them both.

"You should probably make me confess some deep dark secret so we'll be even," Aimee said diplomatically.

"Only if you want to," Emerson replied, looking decidedly dangerous.

"I do. Ask me any question, and I promise to answer it."

Emerson took a swig of Coke. She cocked her head and asked the question she'd been dying to all afternoon.

"I know this is probably none of my business, but did Pamela tell you what happened the summer Hope came here? The summer we fell in love?" Emerson asked.

"Yes, she told me the story."

"Did she tell you about how she used to treat Hope?"

"About having other girlfriends?" Aimee replied.

"Well, yes."

"She did. Is that why you don't like her?"

"What makes you think I don't like her?" Emerson asked.

"Because Pamela told me that you don't."

"It's not that I don't like her. It's that she makes me nervous. The two of them together makes me nervous. They have a sort of connection that continues even now. I don't want her here. I don't like always having Pamela on the fringe of our lives. Every time she calls I get a stomachache, and I pray that I won't ever have to see her again. And now she's here," Emerson blurted.

"I commend your hospitality."

"Like I have a choice," Emerson muttered.

"If it makes you feel any better, she isn't quite the same woman you knew. I'm not saying she's morphed into the perfect partner, but she is monogamous and, consequently, less manipulative. She's changed a lot. The thing with Hope really changed her."

Their conversation ended abruptly when Pamela and Hope came out the back door. Hope smiled at Emerson, and Emerson knew they'd had a bit to drink. Hope didn't drink like she used to. Motherhood had changed her. But tonight seemed like an impossible night not to drink. Emerson had stopped drinking after a bad breakup. She wasn't a militant nondrinker but she saw Hope giving up the scotch bottle as a sign of leaving her old life with Pamela behind. And now, of course, Pamela was back. Emerson took a deep breath and tried to relax.

Hope gave Emerson a peck on the cheek and lasciviously licked her ear. Emerson sighed contentedly. Hope knew just how to alleviate her worries.

"I need to make the salad," Emerson said.

"I'll come help," Aimee offered.

"Great," Emerson said.

Nic looked at Hope.

"One hand of Old Maid and then you have to get cleaned up for dinner," Hope said, getting a beer from the cooler.

Pamela did the same.

"Wouldn't want to ruin a good buzz," Pamela said.

"Never," Hope said and they both laughed.

Emerson yanked Aimee into the kitchen.

"See, I told you the two of them back together is not a good thing."

"Emerson, can I be candid?" Aimee said, taking the head of lettuce Emerson handed her. She looked around for a knife.

"By all means."

"I've only known you for the afternoon, but I think I can honestly say you have nothing to worry about. If two people ever loved each other, it's you two," Aimee said emphatically.

"What about you? Everything good?"

Aimee took a minute to answer. "It could be better."

Emerson groaned.

"It's not my fault," Aimee said.

"What's not your fault?" Hope said, coming in to get Nic another Shirley Temple.

"The state of the universe," Emerson replied.

~ ~ ~ ~ ~

The rest of the evening passed without incident, surprisingly. The combination of wine, good food, laughter, and cute questions from Nic eased tensions.

During dinner Pamela discussed lesbian motherhood.

"This is definitely a new phase in the evolution of lesbianism. Before, children were products of divorce. They were not created specifically for the lesbian couple. There are issues, endless issues, about how these children grow up," Pamela stated.

Emerson stared at her with eyes glazed over and thought that Pamela Severson was once again planning a life that was not her own. Then, as if to contradict what she had told Aimee earlier about no longer being such a savage and having learned tolerance, she did chew-and-show with Nic until Hope tapped her gently but firmly with her foot while Pamela considered yet another angle on motherhood.

Emerson picked up Nic, who looked sleepy and tired, and carried her upstairs. Nic waved good-bye, her eyes barely open.

"We should go too," Pamela said, looking over at Aimee.

Aimee simply nodded, stifling a yawn.

"I'd like to finish our talk someday," Emerson whispered in Aimee's ear as she gave her a hug good-night.

"Because you still have issues," Aimee teased.

"Endless issues," Emerson replied.

They both laughed.

"We'll get you set up to see the O'Malley house tomorrow. I think you'll like it," Hope said, walking them out.

"Sounds good," Pamela said, looking at Hope overly long.

They bade each other good-night. Hope and Emerson watched as they walked down the street. Pamela took Aimee's hand. Hope sighed with relief.

~ ~ ~ ~ ~

"You okay?" Hope asked Emerson as she undressed.

"I'm fine," Emerson replied, taking Hope's head and pressing it against her stomach.

Hope held her tightly.

"You know how much I love you and there is nothing to be afraid of," Hope said, pulling away to look Emerson straight in the eye.

"I know. I just get scared," Emerson said, pulling her near.

Hope stroked Emerson's cheek and kissed her softly. She knelt down before her. Hope smiled as she ran her hands up Emerson's naked thighs and then slowly took her in her mouth, her tongue teasing and gliding. Emerson wrapped her fingers through Hope's hair. Emerson's legs tightened, and she moaned softly. Hope moved Emerson back on the bed and straddled her stomach. Emerson gently entered her, and Emerson's fears about Pamela temporarily evaporated. Benevolence washed over her and she felt clean and secure in the knowledge that Hope loved her more than anyone.

As they fell asleep, Hope whispered, "We're a family, and no one is going to break us apart."

Sometimes Emerson drew her closer and wondered if Hope was a mind reader. They fell asleep in each other's arms, and Emerson dreamed of a world where ex-lovers did not come for a visit.

In the morning Emerson watched Hope sleeping. She felt fortunate — a lucky gal, as Berlin always told her. Seeing Pamela again brought back a flood of memories. About falling in love, about building a life together, about getting the house set up and starting a family. They had stalked the town for just the right house. One afternoon they were walking uptown on a sleepy back street lined with huge elm trees when Hope saw the old homestead sitting in the middle of an immense lawn, with a garden that threatened to overtake the house. It was a turn-of-the-twentieth-century Victorian, complete with turret. The house was vacant, and the curtainless windows looked like empty eye sockets.

"This one's looks vacant," Hope said, surveying the house.

"It sure is," Emerson said, looking at the house dispassionately.

"Is it for sale?" Hope asked, walking toward the house to get a better look.

"No," Emerson replied, beginning to get butterflies in her usually placid stomach.

"Who owns it?"

Hope started up the front steps. Emerson followed. Hope peered in the window.

"Well?"

"Well what?" Emerson said, trying not to look overly familiar with the lay of the land.

"Who owns it, and why don't they sell it?" Hope inquired.

"I own it."

"What?" Hope said, looking instantaneously incredulous.

"It's my family's."

"Why don't you live in it? Never mind," Hope replied.

"I like the studio better," Emerson said.

"Did you ever live in it?" Hope asked.

"Not really. Spent a lot of time in boarding school, remember?" Emerson replied, looking at her innocently.

"Emerson, why are we trying to buy a house if you already have one?"

"I kind of forgot about it."

"How can you forget about a house?"

"It never really seemed like mine," Emerson replied, looking completely ambiguous.

16

"It's beautiful."

"Yes," Emerson said, rocking back on her heels.

"Do you have bad memories about it?" Hope quizzed.

"No. I don't really have any memories. I came home for the holidays. That's it. And usually Dad took me to Katherine's. I spent more time there."

"Do you like it?" Hope asked.

"If you like it," Emerson said, taking her hand. "I just want to live with you. I don't care where it is. The house needs work, though. Want to go in?"

"Please."

Hope smiled at Emerson as she pulled her gigantic key chain from her pocket.

Emerson imagined hiring contractors to fix the place up and then moving into a completely refurbished house. But Hope had other ideas.

"No, Emerson, I want to do the work. Not plumbing and electrical — I am willing to be realistic — but I'd like to do the cosmetic stuff at least."

"Thank goodness. I thought you were turning into Bob Villa," Emerson said, giving her a gentle tap.

"I think it's great you're going to fix up the old house," Katherine said, getting them both a Coke.

Emerson whirled around on the café stool, checking out who was hanging around the café. "Can't we just hire people to do it?"

Hope gave her the look, "I want to make it our own, to touch every part of it, to make it our home. I've never had the chance to do something like this, and I'd really like to."

Emerson smiled at her. "For you, anything." She looked at Katherine, "We're disgusting, aren't we?"

"No, you two are beautiful," Katherine said.

That night as they lay in bed Emerson asked Hope why she'd felt so strongly about fixing up the house.

"I have always lived in picture-perfect places, where

17

everything worked, everything was finished, right down to the furniture and rugs. I never got to pick anything out, to decide what I liked and where it would go. I didn't feel like I belonged anywhere. I'd like to change that. Does that make sense?"

"Perfect sense."

The next morning Emerson went to the hardware store and bought everything she thought they'd need. When she got back, Hope held up some mysterious power tool.

"What's this for?"

"I have no idea. I just thought we might need it."

"Tell me you didn't buy one of everything?" Hope asked, raising an eyebrow.

Emerson smiled.

Emerson got up and crept down the stairs, leaving Hope sleeping. Nicole came into the kitchen, rubbing her eyes and smiling sleepily at Emerson.

"Hey, babycakes, how are you?"

"Hungry," Nic said, rubbing her tummy.

Emerson got the cereal. Nicole got the bowls. Emerson got the milk. Nic pulled a banana from the fruit basket. They did this same dance every morning. They had it choreographed to perfection. They both sighed and sat down to eat.

"Is she still asleep?" Nic asked, through her cereal.

"Yes."

"Can I go look?" Nic asked.

"Don't wake her up," Emerson said, stuffing a spoonful of cereal in her mouth.

"You're dripping," Nic said, handing her a napkin.

"Thank you."

Nic crept up the stairs to peek in the door and gaze at her mother.

Emerson didn't quite understand Nic's compulsion with doing this, but she didn't have any room to talk. She did the same thing. They were both obsessed with looking at Hope. Emerson sculpted her. Nic drew her.

Nic came softly down the stairs. Her little face was pink and glowing. She smiled.

"She's so beautiful, Emerson."

"I know, sweetheart."

They ate quietly. Emerson looked at Nic's drawings on the table. Emerson was proud and flattered that Nic had taken such a shine to the arts. Everyone said that all children were artists, but Emerson saw her own extreme compulsive passion in Nic. She didn't draw to amuse herself. She drew because she had to, because she wanted to get her experience down.

Emerson never told anyone this because she knew they would say she was attributing adult motivations to a mere child of five. That it was nonsense. But Emerson saw herself in Nic. She watched closely. Having a child allowed her to experience her own childhood again. It was like discovering who you were while seeing who you had become. It was the queerest thing, Emerson thought.

"Doing some drawing this morning?" Emerson asked, as Nicole got out her drawing materials.

"I want to make a picture for Aimee," Nic replied, looking serious.

"You really like her, don't you?"

"I think I'm in love," Nic replied.

Emerson did her best not to smile. If Nic thought this was serious, she would do her best to think it so too.

"With who?"

"With Aimee, silly. She seems so sad. I want to make a happy picture for her."

"That's nice, sweets."

Emerson got coffee and toast ready for Hope. She put it on a tray and took it upstairs.

Nicole was drawing out on the porch when Aimee and Pamela came by. Nic flew off the porch.

"Hey, where are you two going?" she asked, looking up at Aimee, who smiled down at her benevolently.

"For a walk, take in the sights, get some exercise," Pamela said.

"Want to go to the quarry?" Nic countered.

"Sure, where is it?" Aimee asked, as Nic slid her hand into Aimee's.

"I'll show you."

"You'd better go ask," Pamela said.

"Be right back. Don't go anywhere," Nic said, possessing a child's innate sense that adults were not to be completely trusted.

"We won't," Aimee promised.

"I think she has a crush on you," Pamela said.

Aimee raised her eyebrows and pursed her lips. "At least someone does."

"Aimee, that's not fair."

Aimee shrugged and kicked the crack in the sidewalk, thinking, I wish you'd tell me how you really feel. If you don't love me anymore then let me go, but don't keep me hanging on.

"Nic, you've got to knock first," Hope said. She was leaning against propped-up pillows with Emerson between her legs.

"I'm sorry, Mama, but I want to take Aimee and Pamela to the quarry. Can I? They said I had to ask. Please."

Emerson rolled her eyes and whispered to Hope. "She's in love with Aimee."

"They're waiting. Please. I'll be good. I promise."

"All right," Hope said.

20

Nic shut the door, looking back at her mother who had closed her eyes and smiled.

"Can you go?" Aimee asked. She was finding Nic a pleasant distraction.

"Yeah. Sorry it took so long, but they were doing it again."

"Doing what?" Aimee asked coyly. She watched Pamela stiffen.

"You know, fucking," Nic answered flatly.

"Young lady," Pamela reprimanded.

"Sorry, making love."

"Do they do that a lot?" Aimee asked. Pamela shot her a look. Aimee shrugged.

"All the time. Floyd says they're nymphos."

Aimee burst out laughing.

"It's disgusting," Nic said, making a face.

"Why is it disgusting?" Aimee asked.

"Because they do it all the time. Floyd says his parents don't do it at all."

"Do you know what *it* is?" Pamela asked.

Ever the scientist, Aimee thought.

"Fucking?" Nic inquired.

"Yes," Pamela answered, looking over at Aimee like she had stumped the kid.

"Of course. Floyd says it feels like going to the bathroom after you held it for a long time, an overwhelming sense of relief," Nic said, flouncing down like a wilted flower. "But I still don't understand why you'd want to do it all the time."

Aimee laughed hysterically, wiping tears from her eyes.

"Don't encourage her precociousness," Pamela said, pointing a finger at Aimee.

"Who is Floyd?" Pamela asked.

"He's my best friend."

Nic led them off toward the quarry, holding Aimee's hand and looking up occasionally while she narrated various bits of town history and gossip.

"How old are you again?" Pamela finally asked.

"Five, almost six," Nic said.

"Five going on twenty," Pamela murmured under her breath.

Aimee smirked. Anyone who could penetrate Pamela's armored exterior was all right in her book.

"We should do ice cream after we're done, don't you think? I'll put it on my account," Nic said.

"And just how do you pay for this account?" Pamela asked.

"With my drawings. Berlin buys them."

"I bet she has quite a collection," Aimee said.

"She does," Nic replied, skipping off to pluck a bunch of lilacs. She handed them shyly to Aimee.

Aimee looked at Pamela. Pamela could learn a thing or two from this little one.

Emerson sat at the counter, sipping a malt. Berlin was looking inquisitive.

"So where's Nic?"

"She went with Aimee and Pamela to the quarry," Emerson replied.

"How do you feel about her being in town?" Berlin asked.

"How do you think I feel?" Emerson said, snarling.

"Nervous," Berlin countered.

"Exactly," Emerson replied, thinking of Hope's successful attempt at putting her at ease.

"What about Hope?"

"I don't know. She hasn't talked about it."

"It's going to be a long summer. Maybe she'll get bored."

"Berlin . . ."

"Yes?"

"I think Nic is extremely infatuated with Aimee."

"What's wrong with that?" Berlin asked, wiping off the counter.

"I don't know. It makes me nervous."

"You're afraid she might be a lesbian."

"Well, yeah."

"Would you be disappointed?" Berlin asked, cocking her head.

"It's this having-a-kid thing. Are we turning her into a lesbian by setting an example?"

"You sound just like your father," Berlin said.

"That's why he sent me off, isn't it?" Emerson replied.

"You got it. Lot of good it did, huh?"

"I shouldn't worry then."

"No, Nic will be whatever she wants. What she sees is two women very much in love. And that's good."

"It's not like she doesn't understand that there's another way to be, does she?" Emerson asked.

"I think Floyd keeps her up on stuff like that. Don't worry, Emerson. She knows."

"All right," Emerson said, not looking entirely convinced. She was definitely going to have to do some research on her own. She hoped Pamela wasn't rubbing off on her. But whenever things made her nervous, she read books on the subject. She found comfort in the written word. If the book told her it was all right, then she would believe it.

"Perhaps there's a book on the subject," Berlin suggested.

Emerson nodded and left, wondering why everyone seemed to know her so well. It was like they were all mind readers or something. She made a beeline to the bookstore.

Hope came in later for lunch. Crystal ran the store in the morning, and Hope did the afternoon shift. That way Emerson could have the morning to sculpt while Hope took care of Nic. In the afternoon they switched. They had decided childcare was a bit like waltzing: Everything depended on the agility and grace of your partner.

23

"She's at it again," Hope said.

"I saw her go," Berlin replied.

"Crystal gave me the reading list. I wonder how long this time," Hope said.

"Lord knows," Berlin said, smiling.

"Remember the pregnancy?"

"A perfect nightmare."

"Amusing though," Berlin said. "I'll be right back."

Hope watched her grab a pad and a towel and head toward Ruthie and Elise. The lunch rush was just beginning. Hope ate her tuna sandwich and thought back to those days.

They were lying in bed. Emerson looked over at her.

"I've got this under control. I've read all the literature."

It was true. Emerson had followed her around for weeks, spouting off every conceivable thing about birth, mothering, and parenthood. Hope had reached her boiling point. She snatched the latest encyclopedia of midwifery out of Emerson's hand and threw it across the room.

Emerson looked thoroughly surprised. She quickly recovered herself.

"Well, I guess that's enough reading for tonight."

"I'm looking for reaction, not complacency."

"What did I do?"

"You're driving me out of my fucking mind."

"But the book said that pregnant women are prone to violent mood swings. The partner is thus cautioned to remain calm and to not further aggravate the situation. The partner is to pretend nothing out of the ordinary is occurring," Emerson replied.

"I want us to be like we used to be."

"But we can't. You're a mother now."

"You make me feel like a breeding machine, like I'm not

me anymore. I'm Hope, remember? I'm the woman you used to ardently seduce on a regular basis. You won't even touch me now."

Emerson looked totally shocked. "But —"

"It won't hurt the baby," Hope said. She started to cry.

"I love you. Please don't cry," Emerson said.

"But you don't desire me anymore now that I'm a big, fat, pregnant woman," Hope blubbered.

"I do. I really do. I just thought . . . You know, maybe you didn't feel like it."

"I'm going crazy. I miss you. I miss the way you make me feel," Hope said, drying her eyes on the corner of the sheet.

Emerson got her some tissue.

"I'm sorry. I didn't know. I guess I thought we'd put it on hold until afterward," Emerson said.

Emerson took her in her arms. She leaned back and pulled Hope on top of her, kissing her gently.

"You're beautiful," Emerson said, rubbing her hands across Hope's protruding belly.

Hope smiled as Emerson slipped inside her. The dry spell was over. Sometimes when Hope looked at Nic she remembered how well she'd been loved in the womb. As Hope got bigger they devised new positions. She would always remember that time with special glee. She felt so much love, more love than she'd ever felt before, inside and out, and to think she had to plead with Emerson to have this baby.

That was their first real fight. First big fight. First fight the town was witness to. There were others later. Berlin took odds on who got her way, and the older town lesbians analyzed and promulgated. Hope found this all rather alarming. But in time she got used to it, knowing that the townspeople got involved because they cared, because they were family. Hope had never had such a large and loving family. And nothing or no one could take that away.

Seeing Pamela again brought back feelings she thought

had gone by the wayside. She wasn't quite the butterfly she imagined herself. Try as she might, the cocoon of her previous life lingered.

In those early days Emerson had some strange tendencies, stranger than those she had now. But Hope had fallen in love with those idiosyncrasies, and she wouldn't wish them away for anything. They had set up house, made love in every room in the house, made love when they were supposed to be painting, plumbing, tiling, building. Finally the house was fit to live in, and life took up its quiet tangential flow. In the midst of marital bliss Emerson decided that she loved Hope so deeply that Hope would surely die of a terminal disease, taking her love with her. Hope swore she was healthy.

Emerson demanded she get a physical. Hope refused, thinking Emerson ludicrous. Emerson packed her clothes and moved back to the studio. The town stood witness. Rumors flew. Katherine went to talk to Emerson. Hope tried to reason with her to no avail. They lived like this for two weeks. Every morning after another sleepless night, missing Emerson's warm body, her soft touch, Hope would go and plead with her to come home, always with the same answer.

"You won't go because you're scared," Emerson replied.

"I am not. I'm fine. I feel fine. I am fine."

"You are fine," Emerson said, stroking her cheek.

Hope melted. "Please come home."

"After you go to the doctor."

Hope made an appointment. Emerson made Dr. Lizinsky do a complete physical. Hope sat on the table while the doctor showed Emerson the test results.

"She's fit as a fiddle, Emerson, I swear," Dr. Lizinsky said, with her hand outstretched on the Bible Emerson supplied. "This is highly unusual."

"You forget who we're dealing with here," Hope said, getting off the table, thinking about holding Emerson naked in her arms.

Hope pinned Emerson against the wall of the doctor's office once they were outside. She kissed her deeply making them both quiver.

"If you don't take me home this minute and make love to me for the rest of day, I will surely lose my mind," Hope said.

The phone was ringing when they got home. Amidst ardent kisses in the kitchen, Emerson picked up.

"Lauren, I can't talk now." Emerson hung up as she tried to hold on to Hope, who was slipping away. "Where are you going?"

"To bed," Hope said. Emerson followed her and picked up discarded articles of clothing from the stairs.

When Emerson got wind of Hope's plan to have a baby, she told her, "You have me. I need to be taught, loved, and mothered."

"It's not the same. Don't you want a little creature that we could bring up together, to help create a wonderful being?"

"Let's get a dog then."

"It's not the same. We could get a dog when the baby gets older."

"No baby!" Emerson said, getting red in the face and stomping off.

"Emerson, wait. Let's talk about it."

"There's nothing to talk about."

Most people sided with Hope, thinking that a baby would be lovely and all agreeing that Hope would be a wonderful mother. They thought Emerson was a perfect heathen for not supporting the idea. Hope remembered that it was Berlin who figured out the true reason for Emerson's refusal and who went to see her in the studio. Berlin had told her the story later.

"She won't die you know," Berlin said.

Emerson looked up. "You don't know that for sure."

27

"It was a fluke and less than ideal medical conditions. Things have changed. It won't happen again."

"I couldn't bear to lose her," Emerson said.

"You won't, sweetheart, but you've got to let her do this. Her life won't be complete without it."

"Why aren't I enough? Why does she want this thing to come between us?"

"A baby is not a thing."

"Creature then," Emerson said, stabbing the lump of clay rather fiercely.

Berlin raised an eyebrow. "Jealous, are we?"

"Yes. She's everything to me. Why can't I be the same to her?"

"Emerson, she loves you, having a family is a natural extension of that love. It's because she loves, because she feels secure, that she wants this child. Because she trusts that you'll always be there."

Emerson looked less black. "You really think so? You're not bullshitting me, are you?"

"No."

"Is that why Katherine and you wanted to have a baby?"

"Yes, and despite the challenges of raising a child, I never regretted a moment. Emerson, you could lose Hope over this. Don't be foolish. She'll do it with or without you."

"I'll think about it."

"Don't think too long."

Hope remembered that Berlin had come whistling in the bookstore that day.

"You're in a good mood," Hope said, not looking nearly so cheerful herself. She missed Emerson. She wanted the baby, but she wanted to have it with Emerson. She felt torn.

"Dammit, Berlin, I want a family. I want to be the kind of parent I never had. I want Emerson to want the same thing."

"You'll get it. Don't worry," Berlin said.

The bell on the front door of the shop rang. They both

28

looked to see who it was. Emerson stood holding flowers, a baseball mitt, and a stuffed bear.

"I didn't know what we'd have, so I brought both," Emerson said sheepishly.

Hope rushed into Emerson's arms, kissing her and crying and screaming and laughing.

Theirs was a tumultuous relationship, Hope thought, smiling back at her reveries, but a beautiful one.

Berlin returned from the kitchen, having placed her order. She leaned on the counter and said, "Do you remember the delivery room debacle?"

Hope laughed, "Not something I'm likely to forget."

"I will have to admit that was classic."

"I knew we never should have let her in the delivery room."

"But Emerson insisted," Berlin said.

Hope smiled as her mind conjured up the scene.

The night Hope went into labor they were having a town council meeting over the zoning of a topless bar on the south side of town. The bar was part of a franchise and had big bucks behind it.

A mixed bag of emotions was tossing about on the floor. The lesbians didn't see the point, except that it would bring in boys from Grover who wouldn't zone one. Dickie Sharp was all for it, and so were a surprising number of other local men. The men from Grover were all for it. They were putting pressure on the local men of Heroy.

Berlin stood up. "Look, I don't think it's a good idea. Topless bars are not part of a healthy expression of human sexuality. A bar like that will bring in weird, hostile men, and we all know where that gets us."

"And just what ya call this dyke shit, fucking perverts," Dickie Sharp yapped.

The crowd of men tittered.

"This isn't about dyke shit, this is about profanity, prostitution of female breasts, and pornography," Katherine said, getting red in the face.

"What do you call that shit Emerson does that's all over town? Nothing but naked women," Earl Holland barked out.

"That's art!" Emerson said, getting out of her chair.

Hope pulled on Emerson's belt, whispering, "Relax, darling. He's just trying to get people riled up."

Emerson looked at Hope and then sat back down, remembering she had a very pregnant woman to take care of, and getting into fisticuffs with Dickie Sharp and his gang would not do. Instead, she glared across the room at the group of men trying to foul the town.

Elise whispered to Hope, "The only reason the men want the bar is because they feel like they've lost control of the town. I heard them over at the hardware store before the meeting. They said they were tired of letting the lezzies run this town. The men from Grover were backing them up."

"They just want a sleazy bar in Heroy so they can slink up here and have their little fun without their wives in Grover knowing about," Hope said. Hope was totally against it. She had tried being impartial, thinking about personal freedom. She knew it was not always an easy thing for a town with a straight population in the minority to put up with gay people in record numbers. They weren't used to it. Perhaps this was their way of standing up for themselves. But if it meant exploitation of women, she couldn't abide by it.

The clamor had grown louder. Dickie Sharp was screaming at Berlin.

"Just because you lesbians see all the tits you like doesn't give you the right to deprive normal, fun-loving people."

"Paying to stare at women's breasts is deplorable. Perhaps if you weren't so disgusting you might find yourself a girlfriend who'd give it up for free. Although I doubt there is such a woman," Berlin said.

Emerson smiled at Hope. "I wish I was eloquent like Berlin."

"You have other talents," Hope said, squeezing Emerson's inner thigh. Emerson flushed.

"Listen, you fucking dyke!" Dickie said, coming at Berlin.

"Yeah, bring that big fat belly of yours over here, and I'll bend you over far enough so you can see that shrunken little penis of yours. Bet you haven't seen it in a while, have you?" Berlin taunted.

Katherine blanched. "Berlin I think you may have gone a little too far."

"Order, dammit, I demand order in this assembly," Mayor Lasbeer boomed, but Dickie Sharp and his group of thugs had made their way across the assembly hall. Mayor Lasbeer gave the sign to the sheriff to intervene. Emerson leapt up and stood by Berlin and Katherine, and Elise and Ruthie Clark. Dickie took a step back when he saw Emerson. She'd kicked him in the nuts one too many times, and her left jab wasn't bad either.

"Look, you ladies more or less run this town. How about letting the boys have some fun. We just want our own place. We got rights too," Earl Holland whined.

"This is something new," Berlin said, "straight people complaining about rights. Yeah, you and your boys got the right to come up here and get your dicks all rattled looking at women with fake breasts, and next thing we know we've got our daughters getting raped in the woods by you same nice boys. You put that club here and I'll see to it the fucker burns down, you miserable piece of shrunken foreskin pretending to be a man."

"Oh my," Mayor Lasbeer said.

Dickie Sharp lunged at Berlin, who simply stuck her fist out. Dickie ran right into it and knocked himself cold.

The boys from Grover congregated and started to rumble toward the women. Sheriff Bates got on the microphone. "Now hear this, anyone of you so much as touches a woman and I'll have you hauled in for assault. We don't hit women in this town."

"But women can hit men," Earl shouted back.

"I didn't hit him. He ran into me," Berlin screamed back. Pushing and shoving started in, and the lord only knows what would have happened had not a loud shriek burst forth. Hope fell to the floor. Emerson leapt over chairs and people, with Berlin and Katherine behind her.

"Katherine what's wrong with her?"

"I think she's going into labor," Katherine said, as she and Emerson helped Hope back into her chair.

"Are you all right, honey?" Katherine asked.

"I think my water broke or I peed my pants in all the excitement," Hope said.

"She's having the baby," Emerson said. She began to hyperventilate.

"Now I want everyone to remain calm," Katherine said, looking straight at Emerson.

Berlin took Hope's hand and led her toward the door. Katherine caught Emerson's shoulder. "Emerson, you need to breathe, you need to help Hope through this. Okay now, deep breaths."

"Isn't Hope the one we should be concerned about?" Emerson said. Sweat broke out on her forehead.

"She's not the one hyperventilating. You're going to pass out if you don't relax," Katherine said.

When they wheeled Hope into the maternity ward, Emerson, Katherine, and Berlin were in hot pursuit.

Hope looked pale and nervous. Emerson looked worse. The closer Hope got to actual labor, the worse the nerves got. Katherine tried to coach Hope, who was doing her best to be a good soldier. Berlin tried to keep Emerson from becoming a basket case. Dr. Lizinsky talked Hope and her entourage through it.

"You can do this, Hope. Just push a little a harder. I know it hurts, but I can feel her head," Dr. Lizinsky said.

Emerson stepped in closer to the doctor. She gulped hard when she saw all the blood.

Hope screamed and pushed, and Emerson fainted. She hit her head on the table behind her and lay crumpled in a pile, bleeding from her head.

"Shit, I knew we shouldn't have let her in here," Berlin said, grabbing a towel and putting it on Emerson's head.

Dr. Lizinsky looked torn for a moment between Emerson and the baby. Just then the baby came out of the womb and into Dr. Lizinsky's waiting hands.

"Is Emerson all right? Oh my god I can't believe this!" Hope said between contorted breaths.

When Emerson woke up she had nine stitches and a baby daughter. Her head was throbbing, but she smiled when she looked over to see Hope holding a beautiful baby girl. Emerson reached her hand out across the twin hospital beds she and Hope occupied. Hope took her hand.

"Does she have everything?" Emerson asked tentatively.

"Yes, she's perfect. Are you all right, darling?"

"Yes. Sorry about that," Emerson said, feeling her head. "Stitches?"

"Nine. You did yourself in pretty good. What happened?"

"A nightmare visitation. I'm all right now. When do we get to go home?"

"Soon, darling."

Hope and Berlin laughed at the memory.

"You were definitely better at giving birth than Emerson was. I remember bringing you both flowers in the hospital. It doesn't usually go that way."

"Nothing has ever been usual about us."

"That's for sure," Berlin said. "You're a good mother. You know that, don't you?"

"Sometimes I wonder."

"You are," Berlin reassured her.

Pamela stood at the mossy green edge watching Aimee and Nic skipping stones across the small pool at the base of the massive gray-stone quarry. It seemed so out of place huddled in the woods, cut off from everything, the earth left alone with its scar. Pamela was disturbed by seeing Hope again, and looking at Aimee now reminded her of all those buried things. Last night they had fought.

"Why didn't you tell me the statue in your living room was Hope?" Aimee said the moment they stepped inside the hotel room.

"I didn't think it mattered," Pamela said, coming down from the drink and feeling the onslaught of a hangover. She was tired and didn't have the energy to fight. She was sick of fighting. She was sick of watching them fall apart and not knowing what to do to stop it. She looked at Aimee hopelessly.

"Would it change anything if I told you I loved you?"

"No," Aimee said, closing the bathroom door and starting the shower.

Pamela lay on the bed and listened to the water running, thinking about times when she would have done anything to be in there with Aimee, days when they were courting but not sleeping together. Aimee wouldn't sleep with her because she said Pamela's reputation preceded her. Everyone on campus knew Pamela got around, or rather had gotten around. She stopped getting around after Hope left her. Losing Hope did something to her, something she had yet to discover or conquer. The same something that was killing the love she had now.

In those early days she found herself quite smitten with Aimee. But it was Aimee who had done the chasing. It was Aimee who had stood in the doorway of her office asking her out for dinner after the conference. Pamela remembered actually blushing like a stupid teenager. She'd been watching Aimee since she took the associate professorship in the fall, through faculty Christmas parties, endless staff meetings, even some joint work they'd done, but she hadn't found the energy or the drive she once had to pursue such a woman.

"Is this going out for dinner, or is this a date?"

"Well, Dr. Severson, if you must know, I rather thought it might be a date. That is, if you are available."

"Then, Dr. Nishimo, I would be most delighted."

They slipped out from the conference early because they were both famished. Pamela didn't think it was for food. Dinner was filled with mild flirtation.

"Why did you ask me out?" Pamela asked.

Aimee choked on her sushi. When she recovered she said, "My goodness, you don't beat around the bush do you?"

"Why now? You've been here half a year and never expressed an interest until today."

Aimee's dark eyes met Pamela's steely gray ones. She weighed her answer carefully.

"Because I didn't trust you. I didn't want to be another one of your girls."

"I haven't seen anyone for almost two years."

"I know. It's not like I haven't tried to get your attention," Aimee admonished. "Finally, I decided if I didn't get the ball rolling —"

"Sink or swim?"

"I tread water well."

"So do I."

When Pamela dropped her off, Aimee said, "Thank you for a most enchanting evening, Dr. Severson." Aimee gently squeezed Pamela's hand, and then she got out of the car.

She leaned down on the door of the car and looked into Pamela's eyes, and Aimee kissed her long, slow, and subtle. Pamela felt hot between her legs, a sharp pain in her crotch. Aimee stopped, stroked her cheek, and said, "I'd invite you up, but I never sleep with people I like on the first date."

The smile in Aimee's eyes, the smooth movement in her hand as she waved, the curve of her neck stayed with Pamela for hours afterward. She'd never before noticed a woman like she noticed Aimee. She felt like she was learning to see, remembering what Hope had said about paying attention, about giving all of herself not just pieces.

Their courtship had been slow but pleasant, like sipping sherry rather than guzzling beer. Pamela remembered having a picnic with Aimee, listening to her reading some important passage from a book. She had run her hand down Aimee's back, brushed her hair behind her ear, looked longingly into her eyes. Aimee had turned and smiled — Aimee told her later that was the moment they fell in love — and Pamela rolled on her back and Aimee kissed her.

Then one night Aimee had made her dinner. They were kissing and cooking and eating and drinking. After they had done the dishes, Aimee pulled Pamela into the doorway of the bedroom.

"I want you to stay tonight," Aimee said, color rising to her cheeks, desire laced in her eyes.

It was a look Pamela knew well, the look of being desired. Seeing it again now was more than Pamela could bear. She burst into tears.

"I'm sorry. I'm so sorry. I can't. I have to go," Pamela said, pulling away.

Aimee knocked on Pamela's door. Aimee looked confused when Pamela opened the door.

"I'm not letting you off that easy. I want you to tell me what happened. I want you to tell me who hurt you like this."

"I don't know if I can," Pamela said.

"Try. Try for me," Aimee said.

Pamela told her the story. She did her best to tell the true version, the real reason Hope got away, the kind of woman Pamela had once been, the way she had hurt her lovers.

"I don't want to do that to anyone again. That's why I have steered clear of relationships," Pamela said, studying her hands.

"You won't," Aimee said, taking one of her hands in her own. She brought it to her lips and kissed it.

"It's late," Pamela said, looking at the gray light of dawn through the open window.

"I should go," Aimee said. "Are you all right?"

"Don't go," Pamela said. And this time it was *her* face that spoke of desire.

"Are you sure?"

"Yes."

They had fallen asleep in each other's arms, and when they awoke they made love. They spent the day making love.

And that's what they should have been doing instead of fighting, Pamela thought. She had opened the door to the bathroom slowly. Aimee, who had been drying off, looked at Pamela and started to cry.

"Damn you," Aimee said.

Pamela had kissed her gently, kissed her neck, pulled her tighter, whispered, "I'm sorry. I didn't mean to hurt you."

She had taken Aimee to bed, wondering if she couldn't somehow make this work.

Aimee and Nic came back up from the quarry. Aimee was holding a bunch of violets and foxglove to add to her lilacs. She was smiling and holding Nic's hand.

"Nic picked them for me," Aimee said.

"Pretty ladies should have pretty flowers," Nic said.

"Yes, they should," Pamela said, taking Aimee's other hand.

Two

Aimee looked back at the house. They had leased the O'Malley place for an extremely reasonable rate. It was an old Victorian house similar to Hope and Emerson's. It was smaller but still conducive to their needs, and it came furnished — a plus. The house looked like the family had walked off and left it without looking back. The Realtor wouldn't say what happened, but Aimee knew Berlin would have all the answers. So she smiled and nodded when the swanky Realtor feigned ignorance, and she signed the lease. As long as there weren't bodies buried in the cellar, Aimee was content.

She sighed rather heavily and wished for the kind of permanence that a house like that represented. It had been there a hundred years and had seen many families grow up and a town evolve around it. Because Aimee's father was a scientist with the government, she had never stayed in the same place for more than a few years.

Was she a drifter in love, too? Was she blaming Pamela for things she felt? Making love last night had been wonderful, but why did she feel so shitty today? Because she fucks you to placate you back into her heart, the demon voice in her head replied. Aimee sighed again and went to find Emerson. Pamela thought it would be better for Aimee to interview Emerson. Less awkward. Aimee didn't mind. She liked Emerson and thought it would be fun to spend some time with the artist-in-residence. She made her way across town to the Third Street Studio, which, as she would find out later, had had a face-lift at Hope's gentle persuasion. The pit had gone posh.

When Aimee walked in the room, Emerson looked up from the piece she was sculpting.

"Hello. Nice work," Aimee said, admiring the piece.

"Thank you," Emerson replied, spinning it around on the stand and looking at it hard.

"Did you know Pamela has one of your pieces in her apartment?"

"Yes," Emerson replied, trying not to look instantly guilty.

"Pamela said she bought it from a gallery in New York."

"She did," Emerson replied.

"Did you sell it to her?"

"No, the gallery did. She doesn't know I know."

"Why is that?" Aimee said, taking a look around, trying to cover her apparent frustration and embarrassment.

"Because when the gallery sells a piece they are under no obligation to tell the artist who bought it. Lauren knew, and she asked me if it was all right."

"It doesn't bother you?" Aimee asked.

"It bothers me, but I felt guilty for taking Hope away from her. It was penance, I guess," Emerson replied, not meeting Aimee's gaze.

"I just wish someone would have told me," Aimee replied.

"Why?" Emerson asked, handing Aimee a Coke she hadn't ask for.

"Because that statue stands for everything I'm not, and obviously Pamela went to great lengths to get it," Aimee replied, staring straight at Emerson.

"Ah yes, the lesbian syndrome of last-girlfriend nirvana."

"Excuse me?"

"Isn't that what this is about? What's making us both nervous? You know, current girlfriend still very much in the clutches of the last girlfriend remembering all the wonderful things that had gone on, things distorted by memory. The past is always so much better than the present. Stupid cultural illusions of what never was."

"Do they know that?" Aimee asked.

"No, but they will after they spend the summer together," Emerson ventured.

"Now there is a sound statement," Aimee said.

"I would have told you about the sculpture if I had known Pamela hadn't," Emerson replied apologetically.

"It's all right. Thanks for playing counselor," Aimee said. "Sometimes I just need the voice of reason."

"Coming from me, that's pretty scary."

"The enigma most often speaks the truth."

"Can I ask you a question?"

"Shoot," Aimee said, taking a swig of Coke.

"How long have you and Pamela been together, and when did you first notice things falling apart?"

"That's two questions."

"I'm mathematically illiterate," Emerson said, looking coyly at Aimee.

"What makes you think things are falling apart?" Aimee replied, equally as coyly, thinking she and Emerson both knew how to work women in their favor.

"Because they are."

"Three years and after the initial isn't-this-grand feeling, something else crept in like a bad smell we can't get rid of," Aimee confessed, feeling the cascade of bad moments, missed cues, groping instances of trying to make that final important connection that would truly make them partners. It wasn't like they both didn't want it to work. Neither she nor Pamela needed another failed relationship. They used to talk about making their love affair work, about making it permanent, about not wanting to leave and start over again with someone new.

"And you think it's you?" Emerson inquired tentatively.

"Shouldn't I?" Aimee replied, thinking she'd dated half the lesbians in New York and left them all for one reason or another.

"Takes two to tango."

They heard footsteps on the stairs.

"I'd better go," Aimee said, setting her unfinished drink down and making for the door.

"Come back soon," Emerson said, meeting her gaze and reluctantly letting it go.

"I shall. You're part of my summer's assignment," Aimee said wistfully.

Emerson arched an eyebrow. "I think I might like that."

"Good," Aimee said.

"Watch out everyone, Dragon Lady's here," Emerson said, as a stylishly dressed woman passed through the door.

"Emerson, I wish you wouldn't call me that," Lauren said.

"Good-bye," Aimee said.

"Remember, we still have issues to resolve as part of my summer's project," Emerson said.

"I will. See ya," Aimee said, turning around.

Lauren sat on the corner of the desk, watching Aimee walk to the door. "What is that supposed to mean?" Aimee turned and looked back, sensing Lauren's eyes on her. Their eyes met, and they both smiled, shyly.

"What's what?" Emerson asked.

"Oh my," Lauren said, watching the empty doorframe.

"What are you talking about?" Emerson asked, picking up her modeling tool.

"Who was that?" Lauren asked.

"Wouldn't you like to know," Emerson teased. "Or rather, why would you like to know?"

Lauren jiggled the stand on which the piece Emerson was working on sat. Emerson, alarmed, steadied it.

"You wouldn't."

"I might. Who is she?" Lauren inquired.

"Interested?" Emerson teased.

"I could be," Lauren responded, surprising them both.

"Buy me lunch?"

"Yes."

"She's married," Emerson replied flatly.

"Since when did that stop anyone anymore? The best women are imported. Isn't that where you found yours?" Lauren replied.

"Are you serious?" Emerson asked, picking up signals from Lauren that she wasn't used to.

"What? Dragon ladies are incapable of basic human tendencies such as curiosity?"

"And spontaneous lust," Emerson countered.

"I just want to know who she is. Why are you tormenting me?" Lauren said.

"I've never seen anyone turn your head before."

"Maybe I haven't met the right one before," Lauren replied defensively.

"Lauren, how old were you when you figured out you were a lesbian?" Emerson inquired, knowing full well the answer.

"I always was one. It just didn't occur to me until I was thirty-three. Why do you ask?" Lauren replied, attempting nonchalance.

"No reason," Emerson replied.

Lauren rolled her eyes. "Lunch?"

"Please, I'm famished," Emerson replied, sticking the modeling tool in the forehead of the piece she was working.

"What's wrong?" Lauren asked.

"I don't want to talk about it."

"Why not?"

"It'll ruin my appetite."

Katherine and Berlin stood outside the American Legion Hall, where they had attended the Lesbian Rotary Club meeting. Katherine could tell that Berlin was crabby because, first off, she hated city politics and, second, she hated Camille Carlye and her insidious influence on the rest of the town.

"I don't know why you come to these meetings if they upset you so much," Katherine said.

"Because I have to know what that woman is up to on a daily basis, and this is where she boldly shows her colors," Berlin replied.

"This is true. She is definitely a town character."

"Prick is more like it. One gigantic prick," Berlin said.

"Technically speaking, women can't be pricks," Katherine replied.

"They can if they behave like pricks," Berlin said, adjusting her canvas hat as a gust of wind blew it straight up.

"Meaning?" Katherine asked.

"She thinks with her nonexistent penis instead of her brain, a typically male behavior. If she doesn't keep her prick out of my face, I'm going to bite it off."

"You've never had one of those things in your mouth, have you?" Katherine asked.

"Of course not. Most lesbians previous to enlightenment do not enjoy oral sex. The kind where you suck on the hotdog," Berlin amended.

"What are you basing that supposition on?" Katherine inquired.

"Statistical information," Berlin stated.

"You've done a survey?"

"More or less," Berlin muttered.

"I find that hard to believe," Katherine said, ever playing the devil's advocate. That was the beauty of their twenty-year relationship. They could tease, joke, and cajole without harm to the other's fragile ego. Sometimes Katherine thought it was nice to be an older lesbian and not have to be concerned with appearances and prejudices and all the worries of the young. It was nice to be in her fifties and coming into herself with a kind of glee she never could have imagined when she was younger. Katherine liked her feisty mate, her life, and the place where she lived.

"Let me prove my point," Berlin said, looking determined as she scanned the horizon for an available bystander. Hope came around the corner with Pamela. Hope was giving Pamela a tour of the town, and they had bought some groceries to get Pamela and Aimee started in the new house.

"Perfect!" Berlin said. "Same age group, similar backgrounds, early-in-life lesbians."

Katherine rolled her eyes. This tangent was quickly becoming more than she'd bargained for.

"Hello there," Hope said as they passed.

"Hold up a sec," Berlin said. "I have a question for you two."

"Okay," Hope said, looking at Pamela. Pamela was slowly adjusting to the relaxed pace of small-town life. It had been a struggle, but she was learning.

"Did you ever give blow jobs?" Berlin asked.

"Excuse me?" Pamela said, trying not to blanch.

"It's all that loud music your generation listens to. I tell you, the end of the twentieth century will be known for body piercing, tattoos, and deafness," Berlin stated emphatically.

Pamela blushed. "Did you say 'blow jobs'?"

"I did," Berlin replied.

"Yuck," Hope said.

"Does that mean no?" Berlin asked, taking one finger and chalking it up on her imaginary chalkboard.

Katherine let out a prolonged sigh. In all the years she'd been with Berlin, she still had a difficult time dealing with her bizarre tangents.

"It means I've never slept with a man, much less sucked on any of his body parts," Hope replied.

"She's a true lesbian," Berlin told Katherine.

"What's that supposed to mean?" Katherine asked.

"She's never slept with a man," Berlin replied with authority.

"And that makes her a true lesbian?" Pamela asked, flipping immediately into her scholar mode.

"Yes," Berlin replied, meeting her gaze with equal aplomb.

"What are the rest of us, false lesbians? Contaminated lesbians?" Pamela asked.

"So, you've given yourself away. Blow jobs?" Berlin asked.

"No blow jobs," Pamela replied. "I can't believe we're having this conversation."

"Why not?" Berlin asked.

"This town has more lesbians living in it than any other place in the world, and we're talking about blow jobs," Pamela replied.

"My favorite subject," Dickie Sharp said, as he staggered out of the Legion Hall. Today was two for ones on Bloody Marys. Dickie had four sets.

"Get out of here, you prick," Katherine said, looking at Berlin. "Now he can be a prick."

"True," Berlin said.

On the way home from the Legion Hall, Berlin asked everyone they met about blow jobs, much to Katherine's

46

dismay. She never should have started this thing. Mayor Lasbeer called later and told Katherine that next time Berlin got a wild hair up her ass to survey people's sexual habits, she'd have Sheriff Bates charge her with disturbing the peace.

"She's just sore at me because she lost at five-card slut last night," Berlin replied.

"Five-card slut?" Katherine said.

"Camille is into linguistic political correctness. *Stud* is too male for her, so I changed it to *slut*," Berlin explained.

"And that made her happy?"

"Not exactly," Berlin replied, lighting up a cigar, which got her a look from Katherine. "I'll go outside."

"Camille is making your life difficult, eh?" Katherine replied.

"I wish she would have kept her academic, feminist, separatist, activist, linguistic fat ass in California where it belongs."

"Well, no doubt as to your feelings," Katherine said.

"No. She's trying to do things to this town that I don't think are necessarily good for it."

"Yes, I know," Katherine said, thinking she didn't have the energy to explore yet another one of Berlin's tangents.

Nic and Floyd were building a wooden jump for their bikes. Nic looked up from hammering. She was now in charge of the hammer, as Floyd had already smashed his thumb rather badly.

"Oh gosh!"

"What?" Floyd asked.

"There she is."

"There who is?" Floyd asked, seeing a woman walking up the street with a box of computer paper and carrying an equally heavy backpack.

"Aimee," Nic said, watching every step she made.

"Who's Aimee?"

"My dream girl," Nic said.

"What are you talking about?"

"I think I'm in love," Nic said.

"You're not a thespian too, are you?" Floyd said, looking thoroughly disappointed.

"It's *lesbian*, dummy."

Aimee walked up to them. "What are you two doing?"

Nic blushed. "Building a jump. It's almost done. Want to watch?"

"I tell you what. Let me go inside and put this stuff away, and then I'll come watch. Okay?"

"Sure."

Aimee went inside.

"Isn't she cute?"

"For a girl," Floyd said.

"I'm a girl. Don't you think I'm cute?"

"You're just Nic."

"I think you're cute," Nic replied.

"All right, you're cute. Can we get this jump finished?"

"Yes, Aimee will be back any minute," Nic said, eagerly getting back to work.

Aimee drank a soda as she watched Nic prepare to take the jump. The O'Malley place was nestled on Morgan Hill, and the street wound at a sharp incline. As Nic took off, it occurred to Aimee that perhaps this wasn't a safe thing for the youngsters to be doing. Shit, some parent you'd make, Aimee thought to herself. At least they have helmets on. They probably do stuff like this all the time, she tried to reassure herself.

Nic hit the jump, and there was a terrible snapping noise. The main brace of the jump collapsed and sent Nic flying head over heels on her bike. Floyd and Aimee ran to Nic. She got up slowly.

"Are you all right?" they asked at the same time.

"Ouch," Nic said. But she didn't cry.

Aimee looked down at Nic's bleeding shins, hands, and elbows. Nic stood there taking deep breaths.

"I won't be doing that anymore today," Nic said. "You won't tell my mom, will you? She'd be really mad. We're not supposed to be jumping."

Floyd shook his head in agreement. Nic and Floyd studied Aimee for a moment, as if trying to decide if they could trust her, since she was a grownup and one of *them*.

"Why don't you come inside and we'll get you cleaned up," Aimee said.

"I can't if you're going to tell," Nic said, standing her ground.

"Nic, you're bleeding. Please," Aimee said.

Nic just stood there.

"All right. I won't tell," Aimee said. Is it any wonder I have lost control of my life when I lose a battle of wills to a five-year-old? she thought.

Aimee sat Nic on the toilet while Floyd watched intently. She got out the hydrogen peroxide and a roll of gauze. Thank god whoever had lived here before was into first-aid. They'd been left a first-rate kit. Aimee still meant to ask Berlin what had happened to the owners. Why had they left everything intact and just bailed out of the place? Aimee sometimes felt like they were guests of someone whom they had never met. Someone who gave them free rein of the house and expected nothing in return. She hoped there wasn't a body buried in the cellar.

Nic winced, but it looked more like Floyd was the one who was going to cry.

"It doesn't hurt. Honest, Floyd," Nic said, taking his hand.

"It looks bad," Floyd said.

As Aimee cleaned the wounds and applied the gauze, she thought about herself when she was kid. She had never cried either. Pamela was the only person in the world who made her cry, but she was also the only one whom Aimee truly loved. Aimee knew she was supposed to love her parents, but something was missing. Aimee looked at Nic and wondered for half a second if it was the same for her.

"Better?" Aimee asked.

"Much. Thank you," Nic said, giving her a hug, a tight, hard, friends-for-life hug.

Aimee smiled and picked Nic off the commode. "You're a pretty tough little comrade."

Nic smiled and whispered in her ear, "It really hurts, but I'd rather die first than let Floyd see me cry."

Aimee laughed, "I get it."

"What's going on in here?" Pamela asked as she walked into the increasingly small bathroom. She looked at Aimee holding Nic. For Aimee it felt suddenly right.

"Nic had an accident," Aimee replied.

"Doing what?"

Both Nic and Floyd stared at her. The moment of truth had arrived. Whose side was she on?

Aimee smiled sweetly. "She fell down."

"Is she all right?"

"I'm fine, thank you," Nic replied.

"I think we just might have some ice cream in the fridge," Aimee said.

"It's raspberry cream for dessert tonight," Pamela said.

"So? I'll get more. Please, let's not add insult to injury, shall we, Dr. Severson?"

"I love raspberry cream," Nic chimed in.

"I bet you do," Pamela replied, narrowing her eyes.

Aimee set Nic down. Nic took Pamela's hand. "My mom says you're really smart."

"Oh, she did," Pamela said, trying to suppress a smile.

Floyd rolled his eyes at Aimee, who had to try extremely

hard not to laugh. Dr. Severson being charmed by a mere child.

Pamela declined to have ice cream with them. She had some work to do, and she gave Aimee a shouldn't-you-be-doing-the-same look. So Aimee, Nic, and Floyd sat at the kitchen table with huge bowls of ice cream. They all smiled mischievously.

When Pamela was out of earshot, Aimee said, "Boy, Nic, you can be pretty charming when you want to be."

"Who, me?" Nic said, putting on her best angelic face.

"Yes, darling. You had mean Dr. Severson eating right out of your hand."

"Uh-huh," Nic said, shoving an overly large spoonful of ice cream in her mouth.

"You should see her with the girls at school," Floyd said.

"What do you mean?" Aimee asked.

"Tammy Lambroski is in love with Nic, and Nic won't pay any attention to her. It drives Tammy crazy."

"Nic, that's mean."

"She's disgusting. She wears frilly little dresses and shiny black shoes and wants to play with dolls all the time."

"Some girls like dolls," Aimee said.

"I bet you didn't play with dolls when you were a kid," Nic said.

"And what if I did? You wouldn't like me anymore?" Aimee countered.

"Well, it'd be hard. I don't like frilly girls."

"Nic!"

"You didn't, did you?" Nic asked.

"No, I didn't," Aimee replied.

"What kind of toys did you play with?" Floyd asked.

"I didn't play with toys," Aimee replied, thinking about her childhood.

"But everyone plays with toys," Floyd said in disbelief.

"No, Floyd, some people have art lessons, language tutors, ballet and etiquette classes."

"Boy, what a bummer," Floyd said.

Nic stuck her entire face into her ice cream. When she came up she looked at Aimee.

"What are you doing?" Aimee said, laughing.

"Making you smile," Nic said.

Aimee got her a wet paper towel. Nic cleaned up.

"Thanks for lying for us," Nic said.

"I didn't lie," Aimee replied.

"But you told Pamela I fell down," Nic replied, confused.

"You did, didn't you?"

"Yes," Nic replied.

"Then I didn't lie. Lying is not a good thing. You know that, right?"

"Yes," they both replied.

"But if it's not lying and it's not the truth, what is it?" Nic asked.

"It's stretching the truth. You fell down, but I didn't say off your bike going over a jump."

"So really you made the truth smaller," Floyd said.

"Exactly. Kind of like Silly Putty. I took the long, stretched-out truth and made it more concise," Aimee replied, wondering if telling small children this kind of secret was a good idea.

"What does *concise* mean?" Nic asked.

"Smaller, like if I rolled the stretched-out piece of Silly Putty into a nice, neat, little ball," Aimee said.

"I get it," Nic said.

"But you two have to promise me something," Aimee said.

"What?" they replied in unison.

"That you won't do any more jumping."

"I think my jumping days are over," Nic said, shaking her head.

~ ~ ~ ~ ~

52

Aimee and Pamela stood on the porch and watched them take off down the hill on their bikes.

"Ever thought about having a child?" Aimee asked.

Pamela scrunched up her face in obvious displeasure. "No."

"I didn't think so," Aimee said. "I'll go get some more ice cream."

"All right. I'll start dinner. Oh, I forgot to get some wine."

"I'll get it."

"Aimee, are you okay?" Pamela asked.

"I'm fine. I'll see you in a bit," Aimee said, doing her best to smile.

Pamela watched her go. Why had she thought that bringing Aimee here was going to fix anything? She had thought that she could somehow woo her back by working together in a place where women as couples lasted for an eon. The problem was, she couldn't figure out why Aimee and she were falling apart. Why was she so successful at pushing people *out* of her life when she so seriously wanted them *in* her life? What's wrong with me? she asked herself. You're selfish, a voice in the back of her head replied. Someone had told her that a long time ago. She couldn't remember who. She guessed it wasn't important. Dinner, the six o'clock news, and those historical records were important. She set herself to task.

Nic flew past her mother.

"Nic, wait! Where are you going?"

"I'm going to take a bath," Nic said, climbing the stairs.

"Now?" Hope asked, puzzled. Usually it was a battle to get Nic in the tub. Five-year-olds were difficult to convince about the virtues of personal hygiene.

"Well, yeah, then I can put my pajamas on and be all ready for bed. I'm really tired."

"It's only five o'clock."

"I know," Nic said as she continued running up the stairs.

Hope heard the water running and started to make the salad for dinner. She got a queer feeling in her stomach. Berlin told her those kind of feelings were commonly referred to as mother's intuition. She followed it and went upstairs. She knocked on the bathroom door.

"Nic, are you all right?"

"I'm fine, Mom, honest," Nic replied, looking down at her scraped body.

Hope opened the door and peeked in. "Are you sure? You're acting funny."

"I'm sure," Nic said, shaking her head with a false bravado.

Hope started to come into the bathroom. Nic panicked.

"Don't come in."

"Why not?" Hope asked.

"I'm naked."

"I've seen you naked before."

"This is different."

"Why?" Hope asked, now seriously concerned.

"I'm older now," Nic said.

Hope came in. "Nic, what's wrong?" Hope looked down at her. Some of the cuts had started to bleed again, and the water in the tub had turned pink.

"Nic! What happened? Oh my god, honey, look at you. You're all scraped up. What did you do?"

"I fell," Nic said, looking down, her face flushing with shame.

"Nic, this looks like road rash. So you fell off your bike . . ."

"I fell off my bike."

"Where?"

"Morgan Hill," Nic said, looking up at her mother.

Hope got the flash of mother's intuition, "You were jumping."

Nic didn't answer.

"Nic, tell me," Hope prodded.

"We were jumping and the jump broke," Nic confessed.

"You know what this means, don't you?" Hope said, staring intently at Nic.

"I'm grounded," Nic replied, lowering her head.

"That's right. One week. No playing with Floyd, no leaving the house except for school, and no watching *The Science Guy*. Now, let's get you cleaned up."

Nic looked like a mummy by the time Hope was done with her. She didn't tell Hope that Aimee had done a much neater job. She didn't want to get Aimee in trouble.

When Emerson got home, she laughed at Nic's new costume.

"It's a little early for Halloween," Emerson said, swooping her up. But when Nic cried out, Emerson set her down gently. "What happened?"

"She was jumping and fell off her bike. She's got road rash everywhere," Hope said.

"And now I'm grounded," Nic said, helping her mother set the table.

"Bummer, dude. I hope you had your helmet on," Emerson said.

"I did."

"Good girl. Boy, Nic, that's going to hurt come tomorrow," Emerson told her.

"It hurts already," Nic said.

"Just wait."

"Have you ever had road rash?" Nic asked.

"Of course," Emerson said, rolling up her pant leg to reveal her scarred knees.

"Did you get grounded?" Nic asked, sticking out a tentative finger to touch the scar on Emerson's leg.

"No, but I should have been," Emerson said, winking at

Hope. "Today is your lucky day, though. I bought you something that might make your incarceration a little more tolerable."

"My what?"

"Your grounding. *Incarceration* means you're being held by the state until they decide what to do with you."

"In prison?" Nic asked, her eyes getting big.

"Yes."

"What did you buy me?" Nic said, getting excited.

"It's in the living room."

Nic flew out of the room.

"She's pretty spry for being all bandaged up like that. What did you do, use a whole roll of gauze?" Emerson chided.

"Okay, so first-aid isn't my forte," Hope said, pinching Emerson, who squealed.

"Is she okay?" Emerson asked, concern written across her face.

"Yes, just scraped up."

"That bike makes me nervous," Emerson said.

"Like you have any room to talk, Rollerblade daredevil that you are."

"I don't let her see me doing those things. I'm much more conservative now," Emerson replied.

"I'll give you that, but all the kids have bikes. If she can't ride her own, she'll ride someone else's. I think she'll be more careful from now on."

"I hope so."

"So what did you get her?" Hope asked, as noises of utter glee came from the living room.

"Come see."

"It's beautiful," Nic said, her eyes shining with pride.

It was a small wooden easel, with paper and a tray of water colors attached. It came with a painter's smock and a black beret. Nic was standing there poised with a brush.

"Well, you know, an artist needs proper equipment," Emerson said.

"Thank you," Nic said shyly, hugging Emerson's legs.

"You're welcome, little one. I was kind of thinking we could fix up the attic so you'd have a place to work."

"My own studio?"

"Would you like that?" Emerson asked, stroking Nic's hair.

"Yes! Then I wouldn't make such a mess in my bedroom," Nic said, looking at Hope.

"Is that okay with you?" Emerson asked Hope.

"Will you promise us to be more careful on your bike?"

"Yes, Mom. I promise."

"All right then.

Nic went whooping up the stairs. She wanted to see how she looked as an artist.

Lauren was debating over the dinner wine to take to Emerson and Hope's. She was staying in town for the night. Emerson hadn't liked the thought of Lauren having to drive back to Santa Fe late at night, so she'd put together a small loft apartment for her in the warehouse. Whenever she was in town, she had her own place to stay.

Over the years, Lauren had begun to spend more time in Heroy, conducting a lot of business from her loft space. Occasionally she bought things for her home away from home to make it feel more like home. Emerson had smiled at this, telling her that the charms of Heroy got everyone in the end. Lauren said she couldn't possibly live in Heroy, too small, too incestuous, too much like one overgrown, out-of-control family. Not for me, she had emphatically told Emerson.

But lately she was finding herself attracted to the overgrown family she thought she could escape from. Ever since Jill's death, Lauren had stridently avoided human contact, except for business, which was why Emerson called her Dragon Lady. She scared everyone off who didn't have something to do with the business of art. She had never told

Emerson the reason why she was standoffish when it came to getting intimate, or that Emerson was really her best friend.

How could she possibly tell anyone that she thought the universe was truly evil for letting the woman she loved get killed by a moving van as it swung wide and hit her lover's car head on. She had held her comatose lover in her arms until they turned off the machines.

Standing there looking at the wine, Lauren thought she would burst into tears again. She'd had to let Jill go without getting to say good-bye. She would rather Jill had walked out of her life forever on someone else's arm. She would rather live with a broken heart, knowing, at least, that Jill was out there somewhere, watching sunsets, making love, taking photographs, than live with the nothingness of death.

Lauren closed her eyes for a moment and took a deep breath. When she opened them, Aimee was standing there looking at the wine. Aimee picked up a bottle and then set it down.

"Shit!" Aimee said, under her breath. She should have asked Pamela what kind of wine. Inevitably, she'd get the wrong one.

"Hey, I know you," Lauren said, immeasurably glad to have a distraction.

Aimee turned around. "You do?"

"We were never introduced, though. I saw you the other day at Emerson's studio. My name is Lauren, i.e., the Dragon Lady," Lauren said, extending a hand shyly.

"I'm Aimee Nishimo. Nice to meet you."

They stood for a moment studying each other's faces, reading the other's underlying misery — and, then again, something else.

"So, wine. What kind when there are so many?" Lauren said, trying to keep the conversation going.

"Especially if you're not a connoisseur. I don't know what kind to get."

"What are you having for dinner?" Lauren asked, thankful for a skill she had always taken for granted.

Aimee looked at her and shrugged her shoulders.

"You don't know what you're having for dinner?"

Aimee put her head down and stuck her hand in her pockets.

"I wasn't paying attention to the menu," Aimee admitted.

"Not good," Lauren replied.

"I know, story of my life," Aimee replied, meeting Lauren's gaze.

"Okay, here's what you do. Get a good white and a good red. Here, this is good and this," Lauren said, pulling two bottles from the shelf. "Go home, find out what you're having for dinner and use whichever one applies and stick the other one way back in a corner of the fridge."

"You're a genius," Aimee said.

"And you're a nuclear physicist," Lauren teased.

"I could be, for all you know."

"But you're not. You're an associate professor of women's studies at Barnard."

"Emerson told you," Aimee said, smiling and obviously flattered.

"She did. She said you were working on a book project. You know, I'm going to the foundry with Emerson tomorrow. Maybe you should come along, get a firsthand look at what goes on. It would be good book material."

"I'd like that."

"So it's a plan?" Lauren said.

"Yes," Aimee replied.

"We'll be by at eight-thirty, if that's all right," Lauren said, looking away. She knew that Aimee had caught her running her eyes over her lovely stomach. It was hard not to look. Aimee stood there in a ratty pair of cutoffs and a short, neon-green tank top.

"Okay," Aimee said.

"You'd better go. Your ice cream's melting," Lauren said. The raspberry ice cream was beginning to drip through Aimee's fingers. They laughed.

"Tomorrow?"

"Tomorrow," Aimee said. She walked down the aisle. Lauren watched her go.

"You're in a good mood," Pamela said, abstaining from commenting that Aimee shouldn't wander around town in scruffy cutoffs and something less than a shirt.

"It's smells wonderful in here," Aimee said, kissing Pamela's cheek and gently squeezing her butt.

Pamela looked at her oddly and then blushed.

Aimee put the wine in the fridge.

"What did you get?"

"A good kind," Aimee said, swinging around. She gathered up silverware and set the table, putting candleholders in the center.

"Do we have candles?" Pamela inquired.

"I don't know. I'll look."

Aimee went through the old hutch in the corner of the dining room and, sure enough, there was a whole box of long, white tapers.

"We do," Aimee said, holding up two candles.

"How nice," Pamela said, gaining momentum from Aimee's good mood.

"Don't you wonder what happened in this house?"

"Not really. I'm just glad we got it."

Aimee lit the candles. "I need to hunt Berlin down and ask about this place."

"They look nice," Pamela said, indicating the candles.

"A little romance . . ."

Pamela smiled, "You never know."

~ ~ ~ ~ ~

They drank both bottles of wine, and Aimee seduced Pamela on the living room floor. Love was fine, love was good, except for the brief moment when Lauren's face flashed in Aimee's mind as she lay between her wife's legs.

Pamela held her tightly, their naked bodies curled together like two spoons. "I love you. You know that, don't you?"

"I do. I just wish we didn't fight so much. We didn't used to fight," Aimee said, squeezing Pamela's hand.

"I know. Maybe having a low-stress summer will help," Pamela offered.

"I hope so. Are you tired?"

"Yes, tired and happy," Pamela said.

In bed Aimee said, "I'm going with Emerson and Lauren to Santa Fe for the day to see the foundry."

"That's sounds fun. Who's Lauren?"

"Emerson's agent."

"You'll like Santa Fe, very picturesque," Pamela said.

"I'll be home for dinner."

"I'll miss you," Pamela said, pulling her close and running her hand down Aimee's stomach.

"I thought you were tired," Aimee said, feeling Pamela's hand slide down her thigh, making her quiver.

"Not that tired," Pamela said, kissing Aimee's breast.

Three

When the third snooze went off, Aimee finally opened her eyes to acknowledge the time. Pamela, of course, was up and off early, going for her morning walk and then over to the county building for records. Pamela detested waiting in lines. She got everywhere early. A point of contention between them. Aimee liked to stay up late and to sleep late. Waiting in line was a perfect place to observe people.

"Shit!" Aimee said, sitting straight up. It was eight-fifteen. Lauren and Emerson would be at the door in fifteen minutes. Aimee gulped down a cup of coffee and got in the shower. At eight-twenty-seven the doorbell rang. Aimee threw on a robe, grabbed a towel to dry her hair, and answered the door hoping to find Emerson. Instead, it was Lauren.

"Up late?" Lauren said, smiling.

"I'm a night owl and really bad with the snooze alarm. I am so sorry," Aimee said, trying hard not to blush.

"Don't be. How about another cup of coffee, and then we'll get going?"

"Where's Emerson?"

"At home. I thought I'd stop here first," Lauren said, sticking her hands in her pockets and rocking back on the heels of her boots.

"Well, let's have a cup of coffee then. Lord knows I could certainly use another one."

"So where's Pamela?" Lauren asked, taking a peek around.

"Out already, as usual."

"I see."

Aimee poured them both coffee, took a few sips, and excused herself to go get dressed, leaving Lauren to peruse the living room.

One half of Lauren's mind was thinking what are you doing here, knowing it was premeditated, knowing she had strong feelings for a woman she'd just met and couldn't get out of her head. The other half was delving into a strange instinctual, lust, infatuation, who-gives-a-fuck, I-like-her, something-clicked mode, that Lauren knew would make Jill laugh.

If Jill were there she would say, That, darling, is how you fall in love. It was in fact how she had fallen in love with Jill. Across a room in a crowded gallery with her partner of nine years. Fallen madly for a taken woman who soon became just as taken with Lauren. Something clicked, and despite the damage they both knew it would cause they couldn't stop. But their affair-turned-relationship wasn't about brief infatuation or pure sexual attraction or any of those other things that characterized marital straying. It was about finding the love of your life.

Of course, she couldn't tell anyone what she was now feeling. And she certainly couldn't say anything to the woman she was having these feelings for. Part of her hoped that by spending some time with Aimee the intensity would diffuse and that Lauren could go on, her emotions remaining in that safe, sane place of mourning, of steering clear of love, because she could never love anyone again like she had loved Jill.

Lauren looked around the quaint living room of the O'Malley place, picking up a book or two, taking in the two camps that were staged there. One stack of books and papers lay neatly piled and organized on the dining room table, while the kitchen table lay strewn with stuff, articles, notebooks, a laptop computer and printer, the last page still hanging out of it, like a large paper tongue. Lauren picked up the papers and read. It was concise and witty. She put them down before Aimee came back in the room.

"So what do you think of the place?" Lauren asked.

"It's okay. Sometimes it feels creepy though. Do you know what happened here?"

"No. Which of the two intellectual workspaces is yours?"

"Which do you think?" Aimee said, getting Lauren more coffee.

Lauren looked at both of them again, and then looked at Aimee. The invitation gave her an opportunity to really look at Aimee. She liked what she saw. Fashionable haircut, thin, medium height, beautiful dark eyes, smooth skin, and a perfect smile.

Lauren knew instantly, "That one," she said, pointing to the messy desk.

Aimee smiled, "Very astute. I do know where everything is, believe it or not."

"I'm sure you do," Lauren said.

"We should probably go."

"We should," Lauren said.

They stood looking at each other for a few seconds longer than necessary.

Emerson sat at the kitchen bar eating her oatmeal and doing chew-and-show for Nic, who was squealing with delight. Every time Hope turned around Emerson looked perfectly innocent.

Lauren and Aimee pulled up front. Nic went flying out the screen door into Lauren's arms.

"Hey, little one. How have you been?"

"You smell good," Nic said, nestling her face in Lauren's neck.

"She's such a charmer," Lauren said.

Aimee leaned over close to Lauren and then said to Nic, "She does smell good."

"You two are going to spoil me," Lauren said.

Nic grabbed Aimee to take her upstairs and show her the new easel.

Lauren and Emerson were talking in the kitchen when they returned. Hope was packing them a picnic basket to take to the foundry. Aimee came in holding Nic, who was taking full advantage of being small and very cute. Lauren stared at them and turned white and promptly sat down at the breakfast nook.

"Are you okay?" Hope asked.

"I'm fine," Lauren said. She had the queerest vision of Aimee holding a child, their child, at some time in the future, looking like she did, smiling at Lauren with love written

65

across her face, and Lauren felt happy and content. And then she snapped back into the moment. Was she losing it?

"Have you had breakfast?" Hope asked.

"No. I never eat breakfast."

"You probably have low blood sugar," Emerson said, pouring Lauren a glass of orange juice and handing her a muffin. "And I bet you didn't eat either," handing Aimee the same stuff.

"I wish you could have seen Emerson before she met Hope. Nothing like the woman you see now, believe me," Lauren chided.

"Let me get my stuff together," Emerson said, blatantly ignoring the comment as she left the room.

"She's ignoring me," Lauren said to Aimee.

"She is."

Hope took Nic upstairs to get her ready for the day, leaving Lauren and Aimee alone.

Aimee reached over and touched Lauren's arm. "Are you sure you're okay?"

"Yes. I just needed something to eat," Lauren said.

"Do you believe in visions or glimpses of what was or will be?" Aimee asked, out of the blue.

"I don't know. Sometimes I think I have glimpses of things, but I'm not certain that I'm not hallucinating. It's weird. They aren't like the garbage dreams we have; they're something different."

"How different?"

"Like they mean something, hold some secret I can't quite catch."

"When do you have them?" Aimee asked, reaching for another muffin and putting one on Lauren's plate.

"Are you sure I need that?" Lauren admonished.

"You're a little too fashionably lean. I'll bet you eat when you're in love," Aimee teased.

"With lesbians, love and food are an almost chronic metaphor."

"Yes, but you didn't answer my question."

"I can't."

"Why not?"

"It's embarrassing."

"How can it be embarrassing?"

"Tell me," Aimee said.

"All right. I mostly have them during astral traveling orgasms."

Aimee burst out laughing.

Lauren blushed. "You asked."

"What's so funny?" Emerson said, bounding into the room with her knapsack and looking around for the picnic basket Hope had packed.

"Astral orgasms," Aimee replied.

"Wow, you two are definitely getting to know each other," Emerson said.

"Darling, I put the basket by the front door," Hope said, from upstairs. They could see her leaning over the side. "Have a good time and be careful."

"We will," Emerson said, running up the stairs and swooping Hope up in her arms. "I'll miss you."

"Ditto," Hope said, nestling her face in Emerson's neck.

"Aren't they disgusting?" Lauren chided.

"No, actually it's depressing," Aimee replied.

"Depressing?"

"Yes, because not all couples are like them but should be. Being in love should be like that, but more often it's not."

"I see," Lauren said, thinking, almost jumping up in wild circles in her mind's eye and then quickly admonishing herself for being gleeful at someone else's expense. She couldn't help it. There was trouble in paradise. She should not feel good about this. She wasn't a home wrecker. Her conscience made her repeat that several times.

Emerson came flying down the stairs.

"Okay, let's go. Lauren, keep Hope busy for a minute, will you?"

Hope came down carrying Nic's backpack and her own bag in preparation for work. Lauren quizzed Hope about life at the bookstore.

Emerson darted into the kitchen, and Lauren saw Emerson shove a bottle of Pepto-Bismol in her front pocket. Emerson and Lauren exchanged a look, and then they all left.

"What was that about?" Lauren asked, once they were safely outside.

"Bad stomach," Emerson said, taking a swig from the bottle.

"Why did you smuggle it out?" Aimee asked.

"I don't want Hope to know. She'll worry."

"How long have you had this?" Lauren asked.

"All my life. Long, boring, story. Let's go."

"Sit up here. You can't hear or talk from back there," Lauren said, as Aimee went to get in the backseat. She folded down the middle seat. Emerson ushered her in.

"Just in case the stomach thing gets worse," she said, taking another swig.

They drove to Santa Fe singing old songs from a compilation of eighties tunes that Lauren had bought from a catalog. When she felt good she listened to the songs and thought about happier times. Lauren made a mental note that Aimee's personal favorites were Blondie songs. Aimee had them doing hand jives out the top of the car, and they entertained many a trucker on the way down. Lauren smiled and laughed, and Emerson was astonished. The Lauren she knew was always deadly serious.

"You are too much fun," Lauren told Aimee.

"You're not bad yourself," Aimee replied.

Emerson made them stop and get another bottle of Pepto-Bismol.

"Two bottles?" Lauren inquired.

"One bottle is to replace the one I took. The other is for now."

They pulled up in front of the foundry which was, as

Aimee would find out, much more than a foundry. It was a veritable art domain, a lesbian utopia filled with women living communally under the benign anarchy of committee decision. Aimee was totally fascinated. Lauren was pleased as she took her around. It had been a long time since anyone had experienced such evident delight.

"I really want to include this in the book we're writing."

"But it's not part of Heroy," Emerson said.

"That doesn't matter. It's about communal living and in this case it's working. The foundry is a perfect example."

"And the town isn't?" Lauren chided.

"No, but the foundry is operating in a more separatist way, which would serve as a juxtaposition to town living where there is a bigger mix of people living together. The town has men and patriarchal rules, albeit modified with lesbian tendencies by virtue of sheer numbers, but here is more of the lesbian-green-world-void-of-men vision put into practice."

"Wow," Emerson said. "We can certainly tell where you went to school."

"What do you mean?"

"Confess. Hope said you graduated cum laude from Harvard. No small task," Emerson said, nodding to the group of women having lunch under a cabana. "Food. We should eat."

"Good idea. You go get us a spot, and Aimee and I will retrieve the picnic basket."

"Sure thing."

"Harvard, huh?" Lauren said.

Aimee stuck her hands in her pockets. "Well, yeah."

"So you're a brain."

"Does that make you like me less?" Aimee asked.

"Should it?" Lauren countered.

"No, but it does scare some people off. It's more about economics and who you know than intelligence."

"I don't scare easily," Lauren said, opening the trunk and handing Aimee the picnic basket.

"This place is really extraordinary. Thank you for bringing me here."

"You are very welcome."

Over lunch they talked with the other women. Lauren watched Aimee's eyes shine with admiration for what these women were doing with their lives and how they came to this lesbian oasis.

"I really think you should talk with Arial. She's technically the matriarch. It was her money that got this started. Right now she's out fund-raising and recruiting," Lillian told them. She was the Birkenstock-granola-bar-earth-mother type as well as the resident potter.

"Recruiting?" Lauren inquired.

"Recruiting funds, women, organizational support, the works. We're much larger than the convert-your-straight-friend-get-a-toaster-oven underground."

"In other words, you're more pervasive, dangerously subterranean, and overall a danger to the status quo as you create your own society," Aimee said.

"Well put, but don't tell anyone," Lillian said, her eyes smiling. "You should come back and let Arial tell you the hertory. Of course, if you were to put it in the book we might have to think that one through as to whether we would make the location known. On the one hand it could be good press, but on the other it might bring trouble."

"True," Aimee said, biting into her sandwich and pondering Lillian's words.

"We'll bring you back to meet Arial," Lauren promised. "I live in Santa Fe, so you wouldn't have to stay in a hotel. I'd be delighted to dust the guest room."

"It's a plan then," Aimee replied, obviously pleased.

The drive back was quiet. Each of them was engrossed in thought. The sun was setting in glorious pink and oranges as they drove into it. Aimee thought about the tour and all the new faces she'd met. It seemed so different from the way women coalesced in the academic world. Here it was comradery and support rather than cutthroat competition where the only bonding that took place was selective and usually involved high stakes. The women in academia were forced to cooperate to endure some crisis or reap some prestigious award. They did not bond or communicate of their own free will.

"It is pretty different," Lauren commented as they discussed the commune while Emerson took a nap on the way home.

Aimee looked at her and smiled. "Yes, it is."

"But you liked it?" Lauren inquired.

"Very much."

"Good."

They pulled up in front of Emerson's house. The porch, where pots of flowers were beginning to bloom, was lit by the light from the living room windows. Sitting in the porch swing and blowing bubbles were Hope and Nic. Emerson gave Lauren and Aimee a hug and let them go on their way. They waved as the family went inside.

They made life look good, Aimee thought. Life full and rich, bursting with warmth and all the mushy stuff we outwardly eschew but secretly crave.

"They look so happy," Aimee said, watching them.

"They are. Do you want to go get a quick beer, unwind a little? I'd understand if it's not convenient."

"I'd love to. You shouldn't anticipate no before the question's been answered. It's bad for your lower self."

"What's my lower self?" Lauren asked. "Some subterranean entity attached to me?"

"The little creature inside us that is always sensitive,

always afraid of looking or feeling foolish, the one that anticipates the blow before it's been contemplated. I imagine it might be something like the soft, white, underbelly of one's ego. You treat it nice so it will feel secure and not ponder every incident as a potentially painful experience."

"Whoa!"

"Get more of an explanation than you bargained for?" Aimee teased.

"Was that something you learned at Harvard?"

"No, B. Dalton's, in the self-help section."

Lauren laughed. Aimee admired her pretty mouth.

The pink neon light of the Saloon shone on the hood of the car, making an eerie pattern. The Saloon wasn't the best bar, but it wasn't a lesbian bar either.

"It's a straight bar," Lauren warned Aimee.

Aimee nodded.

Lauren glided them past Dickie Sharp and his cronies to take a booth in the back. It wasn't as seedy as it looked from the outside.

Aimee knew exactly what Lauren was doing by bringing her here. She wanted to keep her out of trouble. Aimee thought her sweet. She supposed people might think something was going on between them by virtue of association. That was one of the problems of loving women, those boundaries, knowing when friendship turns to passion, always telling yourself she's just your friend and how confusing things get when that happens, Aimee thought. Anyway, it was sweet for Lauren to be concerned for her reputation.

They ordered beer and sat in awkward silence for a moment.

"So tell me about this book thing you're doing."

"Do you really want to hear about it, or are you just being polite?"

"No, I really am interested. I'm always amazed whenever women get funding for any kind of creative endeavor. And

Emerson says you got a contract with one of the big publishing houses. That's impressive."

"That was more Pamela's doing than mine. She's the aggressive one. I like putting twists on things, finding new ways to present stuff, making higher learning an experience to be remembered and not merely trudged through and forgotten."

"I bet you're a good teacher."

"I have my moments."

"I'm sure you have students coming to your office in droves."

"Sometimes I wonder if I didn't secretly become a teacher because I crave adoration. Like some part of me needs to see that line outside my office door. Some days it feels overwhelming, and then I wonder if it's me they see or a lesbian who's out and in a position of power. It's that lesbian thing where maybe you're not really that great at what you do but because of your sexuality it makes you special, gives you that special quality. I don't particularly like thinking that. I want to be me first, a woman, and then a lesbian."

"Not a lesbian, then a woman, then you?" Lauren chided.

"Yes. Don't you feel like that sometimes? How much of a day am I doing things that are exclusive to being a lesbian? Not all my thoughts are lesbian thoughts. I don't have lesbian vision like some 3-D glasses that make the world seem entirely different. I might, during the course of a day, forget I'm a lesbian for a moment or two."

Lauren laughed. "You are so funny."

"You don't laugh a lot, do you?"

Lauren looked serious. "No, I don't. It's nice to laugh. It's nice to be with someone who makes me laugh."

"Does that mean you'll buy me another beer?"

"It's getting late."

"It's nowhere near my curfew."

"All right," Lauren said. "How about we get some to go and drive up to the rim and see the lights. I bet you haven't

73

done that since you've been here." The local boys had noticed their presence. It was time to go.

"No, I haven't. Let's."

"Are you always this spontaneous?" Lauren inquired.

"Just with you."

Lauren smiled.

They pulled off the side of the road and took the path up a hundred yards to a small outcropping. The town hummed and twinkled below them. It looked sleepy, quiet, and calm, like those towns in the fifties' television sitcoms, when life was slow and uncomplicated, or at least appeared that way. Aimee remembered her father sitting in front of those rerun programs mindlessly camping. She had thought it odd that he would watch these shows and find them comforting when the villages in Japan where he had grown up were nothing like those small American TV towns.

They sat down on a set of old camping chairs.

"Do people come here a lot?" Aimee asked, thinking how convenient it was that there were chairs.

"Sometimes. Kids mostly. People hiding out."

"Clandestine romances?" Aimee asked, raising her eyebrow.

"Yes," Lauren said, handing her a beer. "Are you sure Pamela isn't going to be just a little peeved about you being late?"

"I'm my own woman."

Lauren laughed.

"Frankly, she probably won't notice."

"I see."

"So where's your girlfriend?"

"She's dead," Lauren replied matter-of-factly.

"I'm so sorry."

"You don't have to be. It has taken me three years of

practicing that line to say it calmly, to say it without choking, without tears, without an excruciating pain in my chest."

"I know. But what a twenty-question faux pas. I didn't count on that one."

"She got hit by a moving truck coming around the corner too fast," Lauren said.

"You don't have to tell me."

"I wanted to."

"What did you do?" Aimee asked, trying to contemplate what it would be like to lose someone you loved in such a horrid, sudden way.

"It sounds psychotic," Lauren replied. "I've never told anyone this before."

"Try me."

"I went home and I cleaned the bathroom . . . for hours. We used to take baths together, talk, spend time in a busy day catching up. It's weird, but it was something we just did."

"No, it's nice," Aimee said, thinking she had only occasionally showered with Pamela, and it was always sexual.

"So anyway, I just starting cleaning the tub and then everything so I wouldn't have to think. But I couldn't stop thinking. I couldn't stop waiting for her to come home, only she never did. I was a real mess for a long time. I would look out at the world and wonder how I had managed to survive in a universe that allowed such things, that had such perverse disdain for human life. I kept the house just like it was when Jill was alive and sometimes pretended she was coming home, only she never did. I'd throw some of her clothes in the washer and engage in this endless fantasy. Then one day I stopped. I packed her stuff up, and I started the gallery business. Now work is my obsession."

"You're an amazing woman," Aimee said.

"Why do you say that?" Lauren asked.

"Because you're honest about your feelings, and you're strong. See me, I would never confess my pain, and I would have simply engaged in a series of horribly destructive acts and become bent on wrecking everything good in my life," Aimee replied.

"How do you know that?"

"I've done it several times over, and for lesser reasons than the love of my life dying," Aimee replied flatly.

"I'm not as healed as I pretend."

"You don't date," Aimee said, knowing that a lesbian that works a lot is hiding from love.

"No, I don't date. My friends tried to set me up but my heart's not in it. Sometimes you meet the one woman for you and no one else can hope to compare."

"Know that one."

"Who?"

"Hope is Pamela's one and only. I can't compare. But Hope is Emerson's one and only, so the circle gets worse."

"But Hope isn't Emerson's one and only. Angel was. Don't get me wrong, Emerson loves Hope deeply, almost to the point of obsession, but the one that got her the most was Angel."

"What happened?"

"Disappeared off the face of the earth. Emerson came home one night and she was gone. No note, no phone call, nothing. She had just packed a few things and left town. Really did Emerson in."

"Yikes!"

"You said it."

"One more beer and then we'll go?" Aimee asked. She was actually enjoying herself. It was nice talking to Lauren and looking at the lights and feeling like she was on vacation.

"Sure. So is Pamela your one and only?" Lauren asked, trying hard to seem extremely casual as she handed Aimee another of the beers, which were starting to get warm.

"No. I haven't met my one and only. Maybe the theory doesn't pan out for everyone. Maybe some people just get who they get and that's it."

"Let's hope not," Lauren said.

~ ~ ~ ~ ~

Lauren drove Aimee home and stopped the car out front. "I had a really nice time today and tonight, and I want to thank you."

"You did?" Aimee teased.

Lauren looked at her. Aimee wanted to take her in her arms and hold her tight, make the pain and hurt go away.

"I did too. More fun than I've had all summer. You're not the Dragon Lady Emerson makes you out to be."

"Oh, I have my days. You'd better go. I think someone's waiting for you," Lauren said, as they watched the curtain move.

Aimee got out. She turned back on the stairs and waved, lingering a moment. She opened the door and walked smack into Pamela.

"Shit! You scared me," Aimee said, barely recovering her balance.

The dining room table, complete with candles, was set for dinner. Aimee knew she was in trouble. She never does stuff like this, Aimee thought. Go figure with women.

"I'm sorry I'm late, and I obviously fucked up dinner."

"Where were you? I called Hope's and Emerson answered. She'd been home for hours."

"I went for a drink with Lauren," Aimee said, trying hard to not slur. Standing there under the heat of inquisition she felt drunk. She was drunk. Yes, she thought, I am certifiably three sheets to the wind. I wonder where that metaphor came from and how it came to mean drunk? her rambling mind pondered.

"A drink?"

"All right, a few drinks, several drinks," Aimee admitted.

"You could have at least called," Pamela said.

"I didn't think I was going to be that long."

"I thought you said you'd be home for dinner," Pamela replied.

"I'm sorry," Aimee said.

"Are you?"

"Yes."

"So what's she like?" Pamela asked nervously as she heard the other woman's car drive off.

"Who?"

"Lauren . . . the woman you just spent most of the day with and half the night."

"Nice, very nice," Aimee replied.

"I see."

Aimee was tired, tired of the inquisition, tired of standing there feeling like she was sixteen and had exceeded her curfew.

"I'm going to go lie down."

"What about dinner?" Pamela asked.

"I don't think I could eat."

Pamela sat at the table alone. Aimee coming home drunk and disinterested reminded her of the night when Hope came home after drinking half a bottle of scotch to tell her she had fallen in love with Emerson. She had tripped over the coffee table, sending everything on it flying. While cleaning up the mess, both of them on their hands and knees, Hope had told her. She remembered sitting back on her haunches, holding the head of the now broken wooden cat, stunned at what she was hearing. Hope spent the rest of the evening puking while Pamela sat holding that stupid wooden head and crying.

In the morning when Pamela awoke on the couch, she thought maybe she had dreamed the whole thing, but there was the decapitated cat's head and Hope standing at the door with a duffel bag, crying and saying she was sorry, and then was out the door. Pamela went outside and tried to stop her, but Hope simply said I can't, I just can't. And that was it. Walked out of her life, moved away, leaving Pamela with a void she didn't know how to fill. Even with Aimee she wasn't sure she had done what Hope told her, given all of herself, and Pamela knew this was the root of their problems. Aimee knew too. Was Lauren already giving Aimee something Pamela couldn't supply?

Pamela went into the bedroom to find Aimee lying facedown, passed out on the bed with her shoes on. Pamela rolled her over and took her shoes off. She started to undress her, and Aimee opened her eyes and looked up, still hazy from drunken sleep.

"Are you trying to take advantage of me, Dr. Severson?"

"No, ma'am, I just wanted to make you more comfortable," Pamela said, continuing to pull off her shorts.

"Come here," Aimee said.

Pamela crawled into bed with her and let Aimee hold her until they both fell asleep.

Lauren was up and already working when Emerson strolled in. The room was beautifully decorated in a tasteful, lean, and elegant way. Lauren had made her loft apartment worthy of a magazine cover in the space of six months. Emerson put her hands on her hips and studied the room like she always did when she came to see Lauren.

"How come your place looks so good and mine still looks like such a shithole? I've been here a lot longer. I even used to live here."

"Pottery Barn," Lauren replied.

"What?" Emerson said, catching the catalog Lauren tossed at her.

Lauren had simply ordered everything out of the Pottery Barn catalog. It was simple, fast, and required little effort. Some anonymous interior designer had designed the space, and Lauren had paid for it. Lauren's good taste was only in knowing what she liked. She had looked at a photo and ordered. Direct gratification.

If only love were that easy. Lauren had spent the night dreaming of Aimee, which she knew wasn't good. She couldn't get the woman out of her head. She lay in bed while the sky turned from gray to blue, imagining what it would be like to go grocery shopping with a woman she had met two days ago. What would Jill think? She would say, But, darling, you fell in love with me in an afternoon. And she would have been right.

But what about the women she'd run from these past years, nice women some of them, women she couldn't bring herself to like, love, or even fuck. Jill would have laughed about that, too. You, darling, she would have said, the one who could never get enough, the one who would rather spend the day in bed than do any other thing, the one who defined heaven as the place between her lover's legs. But that was only with you, Lauren said to dawn's quiet room. She swore someone whispered, Couldn't it be so again?

Lauren looked up and smiled at Emerson.

"Now that you know my secret to decorating . . ." Lauren said.

"I'm not nearly so impressed," Emerson said, putting the catalog down on the Pottery Barn dark brown desk.

"What's really on your mind?" Lauren asked, knowing Emerson didn't usually visit during her studio hours. Now that she was a parent, time was more precious and ultimately more of a commodity.

"Pamela called to discover Aimee was with you long after you dropped me off," Emerson replied.

"I see."

"Just thought you should know."

"Thank you," Lauren said quietly.

"She's a nice woman," Emerson replied.

"Very."

"You two seemed to have hit it off."

"We have," Lauren said, feeling her heart begin to pound. She felt herself begin to panic at the thought her secret attraction for Aimee was out in the open.

"You're my friend, Lauren. Please be careful. I don't want you to get hurt."

"I won't."

"Okay," Emerson said, leaving.

Lauren called directory assistance to get Aimee's number. It wasn't hard. She simply asked Ethel the new number for the O'Malley place. The hard part was trying to call. She couldn't. She went out for a walk and ran into Nic, who had come screaming around the corner on her bike.

"And what have you been up to, little one?" Lauren asked, glad for the distraction.

"Aimee was reading me a story at the library. She's supposed to be working, but she said I could visit for a while," Nic explained.

"What story did she read you?"

"*The Poet and the Donkey*."

"Did you like it?" Lauren asked.

"Loved it!"

Lauren watched her ride off and then hightailed it to the library without a qualm. She knew she should feel a pang of conscience, but seeing Aimee was more important. She found her on the third floor after an overtly nonchalant but inwardly frantic roaming of the first and second floors. Her heart leapt when she saw Aimee sitting behind a stack of books. She stopped for a moment and watched Aimee work, already sensing that she was beginning to experience moments and that remembering them was going to be important.

She thought about the first time she had met Jill for a clandestine lunch. Jill had been at the café already, and Lauren had stopped on the street to watch her before she went in, like she was memorizing that particular point in time because later it would mark the beginning. The green suit Jill had worn, the way her long dark hair was tied in loose braid, her small, round sunglasses hanging precariously at the end of her elegant nose, how she gazed over the top of them to

81

more fully engage Lauren with her startling green eyes. Jill was beautiful. Sometimes when her image would fade and Lauren needed a reminder, she'd get the photo album out and amaze herself that this incredible woman had loved her, had left another woman for her.

"Are you just going to stand there and ignore me?"

Lauren's revelry was broken.

"I was looking for you."

"You were."

Lauren sat across the table from Aimee, who moved the mountain of books so they could see each other while they talked.

"I didn't get you in trouble last night, did I?" Lauren asked.

"No, you didn't. I could have been cited with a misdemeanor for being inconsiderate, but I wasn't. No need to worry," Aimee answered.

"Emerson made it a point to come tell me that Pamela called the house."

"There is a certain disadvantage to living in a small town," Aimee said.

"I see you are already picking up on the social evils of everyone knowing everything."

"We didn't do anything wrong."

"I know," Lauren replied, feeling momentarily guilty for not having a completely pure conscience about some of her feelings toward Aimee.

"Does that mean we might have lunch together? I'm famished."

Lauren blushed slightly. "I'd like that."

"Where's a good place?" Aimee asked.

"What kind of food do you like?" Lauren countered,

quickly going through her mental files of memorable places to eat.

"Surprise me."

Lauren smiled, "All right."

They drove to Taos.

When Aimee saw them leave the city limits and hit the highway, she asked, "You're not hiding me are you?"

"No, I'm kidnapping you," Lauren teased.

"This could be interesting," Aimee said, raising a seductive eyebrow.

Lauren looked serious. "I'm not hiding you. I just want to go to a good French restaurant, which happens to be in Taos."

"Okay," Aimee replied.

"You like French food, right?" Lauren asked, suddenly alarmed she'd chosen the wrong restaurant.

"Hate it."

"You do?" Lauren said, distraught and ready to make a U-turn.

"I like food in general. And I am quite fond of French food."

Lauren pinched her.

"Ouch!"

"You deserved it."

"I did," Aimee said.

They settled back and listened to music with the top down on the car. The amazingly blue New Mexican sky was like a giant bowl with a mountain motif on its edge.

"I can't believe I didn't want to come here," Aimee said.

"Here?"

"New Mexico. Pamela had to twist my arm and threaten breach of contract if I didn't come. Like I want to spend my summer with her ex-girlfriend in some big redneck wasteland. I had no idea it was this beautiful," Aimee said.

"There are some places here that make you believe in God and paradise, like little coves of heaven stuck in places no one goes."

"Maybe you'll show me one of those glimpses of heaven some day."

"I'd love to."

Hope's bookstore had the good or bad fortune of being located across from the library. If a customer didn't like the price of the book, she could trot across the street and borrow it at the library. However, if the book was out or the library didn't have it, Hope made a sale. The bookstore was a shoo-in for the gay and lesbian books the library didn't have. And as everyone told her, the magazine section at the library was horrible because Mrs. Wheelwright was old and had even older ideas about reading material. Between modern literature and up-to-date magazines, Hope was in a good spot.

Pamela walked in as Hope finished putting together the new window display. She was doing a display on women of the left bank with Gertrude Stein, H. D., Natalie Barney, and the rest of the group.

"It looks good," Pamela said, standing back and taking a hard look.

"You think so?" Hope asked, straightening one of the books that was tilting precariously to one side.

"Yes."

"You and Aimee got me thinking about women's history, so I thought I'd do some promotion. Actually, you've got the whole town excited. Are you ready to start doing the interviews?"

"Yes. I thought I would leave you with a sign-up sheet, see what kind of response we get, and go from there," Pamela replied.

"That's sounds great," Hope said, as she caught Aimee and Lauren leaving the library together out of the corner of her eye. She took Pamela's elbow and led her toward the back of the store. "Let's go out back and have some iced tea and talk.

You've been so busy I don't feel like we've had a chance to catch up."

"Sure," Pamela said, obviously pleased.

They sat in the wooden rockers on the red brick patio beneath a large, wispy, sumac tree. Hope brought them out two glasses of iced tea. Pamela sat admiring the flower garden and the oasis that Hope had created behind the bookstore. She always had a way of taking a spot no one would think of and making it a place of harmony and beauty, someplace to sit quietly, to think, or to read and make yourself feel better about the world. When they had lived together in the loft apartment, Hope had taken a corner of the roof and turned it into a garden paradise. She had found an old wooden library ladder and they had used it to climb out the skylight to get to the garden. No one knew it was there. One bright sunny spring morning they had made love up there on a blanket beneath a perfect blue sky.

"What are you thinking about?" Hope asked, watching Pamela's face as a slow smile crept across it.

Pamela blushed.

"Must have been something nice," Hope teased.

"It was," Pamela said.

"Share then," Hope prodded.

"I can't."

"Is it about us?" Hope coached.

"Yes."

"Then you can share because I was there with you. It's not exactly a secret."

"All right. Do you remember that time we made love on the roof in the wonderful garden you made?"

Hope smiled. "Yes, I remember. It was very nice."

"It was very nice."

They looked at each other and smiled. They both said "very" at the same time, laughing.

"Pamela, are you happy?" Hope asked, trying to capitalize on Pamela's good humor.

"I don't know," Pamela answered honestly.

"Do you love Aimee?"

"Yes. But I keep thinking how you told me I would have to learn to give myself to people. Not to keep things inside that needed to be said and shown."

"And you're not doing that."

"I don't think I know how."

"Why do you find it so difficult?"

"Because I'm emotionally barren . . ." Pamela ventured.

Hope didn't say anything to the contrary. Instead, she looked at Pamela quizzically and then got them more iced tea.

"So you agree?"

"Pamela, what happened to you?"

"I lost you."

"You can't blame everything on that. You let me go long before I left," Hope said. "And by the looks of things you're doing the same thing to Aimee, who is going to leave you in turn if you don't get it together."

Pamela nodded and studied her hands as they sat helplessly cradled in her lap.

"You have to tell people that you love them, that you care, and then you have to show them. You can't just think it and then go around pretending the people you love are supposed to know it and never have the audacity to ask for a small crumb of affection. And fucking their brains out does not count as intimacy."

Pamela burst into tears. Hope was stricken. She hadn't anticipated this.

"I have to go," Pamela said, getting up suddenly.

"Pamela wait!"

She was out the door before Hope could stop her.

~ ~ ~ ~ ~

Emerson found Hope on the porch drinking a scotch and going through a photo album.

"What are you doing?" Emerson asked, sitting next to her.

"I'm trying to figure out why my ex-girlfriend is such an emotional invalid," Hope said, pursing her lips and flipping another page in the photo album she had balanced on her lap.

"Did you have a fight?" Emerson asked, sitting down next to her and looking at the photos. She'd never seen them before. They had come out of a box of Hope's previous life that had gotten shoved in the attic.

"What makes you think we had a fight?"

"You have that look," Emerson said.

"What look?"

"That I-finally-said-what's-on-my-mind-she-didn't-take-it-well-and-now I-feel-bad-for-being-honest look."

"You got it," Hope said. She took a drink and flipped another page.

"What happened?"

"She came to the store, and we were admiring my new window display. I saw Aimee and Lauren leaving the library together. I wanted to distract Pamela, so we went out back and had tea. One thing led to another, and I told her what I thought about her inability to connect with people. She burst into tears and left."

"Did Pamela see them?" Emerson inquired.

"I don't think so," Hope said.

"Thank goodness."

"They like each other, don't they?" Hope said, beginning to put puzzle pieces together in her head.

"I think so."

"This is not good," Hope replied.

"That depends on your perspective."

"Meaning Lauren is an extremely nice woman in need of someone decent to love, and Aimee deserves someone just like her," Hope said.

"Exactly. So you're not still in love with Pamela are you?"

"No. In fact, I'm kind of angry that she is here, that she is depending on me to fix her fucked-up relationship. I care

87

about her, but I can't help being on Aimee's side because Lauren is nice and Pamela will never be that kind to Aimee, because, it's like she said, she's emotionally barren. I don't know what happened to her to make her this way. She thinks my leaving did it. But she was always like that. I was in love with you before I could stop myself because I was so empty," Hope said.

"I'm glad I filled you up. Now tell me about these photographs," Emerson said, looking at a much younger version of Hope in someone else's arms.

"Palm Beach Women's Festival giving a talk about feminism and the role of the lesbian in the women's movement."

"Did you have fun?"

"Fun?" Hope looked at her quizzically.

"Fun. It was a vacation, right?"

"There were no vacations with Pamela. There was work and more work."

"Maybe Aimee is having her own vacation."

Hope nodded.

"What do you think of the food?" Lauren asked, as Aimee devoured her lunch.

"It's wonderful," Aimee said.

"Another bottle of wine?"

"Only if you'll take advantage of me," Aimee teased.

Lauren blushed.

"I was just kidding."

"I know," Lauren said.

"I'm not usually like this," Aimee said.

"Like what?"

"So straightforward, so open with people . . ."

"Usually you're more reserved," Lauren said, trying to help out with the confession. It was, after all, her confession as well. How could she tell anyone that she felt perfectly at ease, felt like she had known Aimee for years when they had only just met. Perhaps it was this confessing deep secrets to each other that took them places most people hardly ever got to despite their long years of acquaintance.

"Well, yes."

"It's okay, really. I feel the same way. It doesn't make sense. But good things almost never do."

"I love your explanations."

Lauren got them another bottle of wine. They both admired the intense blue sky and the subtle beauty of the town. It was a perfect day, and they were having the perfect lunch.

"So tell me about your first girlfriend."

"Only if you'll do the same," Aimee said, pouring them both another glass of wine.

"I was in college, my first semester. We worked together at the library. Now that was a gas. We used to play hide-and-seek down in the catacombs part where they stored the old books. I suppose that was how it all started. Then we began studying together, and one thing led to another."

"You've always been a little wild," Lauren teased.

"Me wild? Never. Wait until you meet my friends the triplets. That's where we get wild. Pamela doesn't know they're coming, but I think you'd like them."

"Pamela doesn't like them?"

"What do you think?" Aimee said.

"I don't really know her," Lauren hedged.

"But you do. Hope and Emerson have told you things."

"Yes, but their point of view is bound to be slanted," Lauren replied, trying not to look guilty for knowing things that Aimee and not other people should have told her.

"I'm sure they gave a fairly accurate rendition."

"And what happened after the one-thing-led-to-another?" Lauren asked, trying to envision a younger, wilder Aimee falling in love for the first time.

"I got straight *C*'s instead of my usual *A*'s, and my father was furious. He couldn't understand how I could be studying all the time in my room with Emily and get such poor grades. I didn't have the heart to tell him we were studying every inch of each other's body's and not sociology, biology, and psychology, although I suppose making love is all those things wrapped up into one glorious orgasm," Aimee said, laughing.

"Do your parents know?"

"Yes, that's how I ended up at Harvard. My father found me between Emily's legs one afternoon, and I went from Barnard to Harvard in a hurry. He didn't want me going to a college full of dykes. Packed me up and shipped me off. My father wanted me to go to Harvard anyway, and I had given him the perfect excuse. I still saw Emily for a while after that, but you know how first loves are. More infatuation than anything else. She wanted to get an apartment together and work our way through school. But I guess I was too much of the brat class to go for that. I'd seen too many people struggling to pull off self-supported education. It didn't look fun, and besides there were even more dykes at Harvard then Barnard. Do you think I'm awful?" Aimee asked, taking in Lauren's bemused expression as horror.

"No, it's good you got to play around, get it out of your system."

"Why did you have that funny little grin?"

"Because Jill was my first love."

"Really?" Aimee said incredulously.

"Is that such a surprise?"

"Well, yes. Here I am saying you know how first loves are, and yours turned out to be something precious."

"She was my first lesbian love. I was married before."

If Aimee had been eating she would have choked. As it was, it took great effort not to spit her mouthful of wine in every direction.

"Married?"

"Yes. Now you're surprised."

"Yeah."

"You can't assume all lesbians were always lesbians," Lauren teased.

"I know. I forget that sometimes. There aren't as many married lesbians as there used to be."

"Are you implying I'm old-fashioned?" Lauren chided.

"No, it just took me for a loop. I can't imagine you married. Were you married when you met Jill?"

"Yes."

"That must have been sticky."

"A little, but it turned out all right in the end . . . almost all right. Jill dying certainly put a glitch in the happy ending."

"I'll say."

"Don't you want to know what happened?"

"Yes. It just feels so delicate when a relationship ends with death. I don't know how to handle it."

"You've never known anyone who has died?" Lauren asked.

"Not yet."

"You're squeamish."

"I am," Aimee said, avoiding Lauren's gaze.

"It's all right. Death isn't catching."

"Unless Pamela finds out about lunch," Aimee said.

Lauren looked immediately alarmed.

"I'm kidding. She's not violent. Well, there was that little shoving match outside Macy's once, but that was more like trying to get the other one out of the way."

"Out of the way of what?"

"A bouquet of dead roses I had in the passenger seat of my car. They needed to be thrown out, but they were mine to throw out and Pamela was attempting to put an end to my nonsense."

"Nonsense?" Lauren asked, thinking Aimee more an enigma than she could ever have imagined.

"Every time Pamela would do something to make me angry or hurt my feelings, instead of talking about it she'd give me a dozen red roses and expect absolution. The first couple of times that flies, but after a while the sight of a dozen roses made me nauseous. I have come to positively hate them."

"All flowers or just roses?" Lauren asked, making a mental note never to send roses.

"Just roses, and I used to love them. So anyway, one day I got fed up and left the roses in the car and let them rot and kept them there as a reminder to both of us that this wasn't working. We got into an argument downtown, and I said something flippant, like, What are you going to do, send roses? and that set it off. But a kindly police officer made us see the error of our ways. He pretty much said stop it or we could fight all we wanted downtown behind bars."

"I take it she doesn't send flowers anymore."

"You got it. Now tell me about this husband of yours and how you left him for another woman."

It was late afternoon when Lauren and Aimee pulled into town. The sun was shimmering over the top of the old oak and maple trees that lined the square in front of the library. When Lauren dropped Aimee off, she wondered if it would be all right to call or if that would be asking too much. Aimee solved the problem.

"I'm going to go through withdrawal with you being in Santa Fe for the week. I don't suppose you could call and break the tedium of small-town life for me?"

"I'd love to," Lauren said.

As Aimee watched Lauren drive off, she suddenly remembered she hadn't given Lauren her phone number, and then one of those bubbling kind of nuances told her she already had it. Riding her bike up the hill in the fading twilight, she tried to picture Lauren falling in love with Jill, how they had their first clandestine lunch, and how a later

92

lunch led to making love all afternoon. But it was the aftermath that made them see how much they really meant to each other. Lauren survived an enraged, insulted, and hurting husband. Despite odds and difficulties, Lauren and Jill needed to be together. And they were until the untimely truck incident. That was what Lauren called it: the untimely truck incident. It probably had taken a lot of therapy to get to those terms.

Aimee left her bike unlocked on the front porch. She still felt it a novelty to leave a bike unlocked, that there were places small enough that stealing a bike meant moving out of town with it. Not very convenient. Thieves, Aimee had discovered, were adamant about convenience.

She could hear the printer screeching across the page. Pamela was pacing back and forth, chain smoking, and obviously deep in thought. Aimee went to the kitchen for a glass of water. Her afternoon hangover complete with dehydration was kicking in. Too much wine at lunch, she thought, but ever so much fun. She smiled. When she turned around, Pamela was standing in the doorway.

"How was your day?" she asked.

"Good. And yours?"

"It was okay. Never get as much done as I'd like. Want to go grab a bite to eat?" Pamela said.

"Actually, I think I'll go lie down. I have a screaming headache. I could make you a sandwich," Aimee offered.

"No, I'll grab something at the café. You go rest. I'll see you later, okay?" Pamela said, kissing Aimee's cheek.

"Is anything wrong?"

"No, not at all. Just concentrating," Pamela answered, heading toward the door.

Aimee plunked down on the couch. She didn't remember falling asleep, but she awoke when Pamela came back with dinner. She sat up and rubbed her eyes, trying to focus. It was dark, and she knew Pamela had been gone a long time.

"I went for a walk," Pamela replied, sensing Aimee's

question. "I got you a sandwich too. I was looking at the paper. *Who's Afraid of Virginia Woolf?* is on television tonight. Want to watch it?"

"Sure."

"Are you hungry?" Pamela asked, touching Aimee's cheek.

"Famished," Aimee said, smiling.

"Good."

Pamela fell asleep halfway through the movie with Aimee's arms wrapped around her. She looked so soft and innocent, so vulnerable when she was sleeping. What had happened to make her such an impenetrable woman? Pamela went for walks when she was upset, but she seldom told Aimee what was wrong. She dealt with it on her own and came back with her own conclusions. Aimee hated that, but then Pamela saw Aimee's expression of emotion as a sign of weakness, making her feel guilty for crying or screaming because Pamela thought she was overdone and slightly banal for showing her feelings.

Aimee sighed heavily, thinking of Lauren at lunch and the times she looked vulnerable and unable to hide it. She clicked off the television. She woke Pamela and together they went to bed. Pamela sleepily snuggled up to Aimee. For the first time it crossed Aimee's mind, does she know who she's with? Aimee answered her own question. Do I know who I'm with? Does anyone really know anyone despite all the so-called intimate moments we spend with each other? Like today, Aimee thought. Lauren and I shared our history in the beginning, as Pamela and I did, and then started hiding parts of one's self again. It's the nemesis of relationships. Aimee closed her eyes and listened to Pamela's even breathing.

Pamela got up early, left Aimee a note taped to the coffeemaker, and went walking. She knew where she would end up, but she prolonged her arrival mostly because she knew the bookstore didn't open until nine. She also knew it was Crystal's day off so Hope would be in earlier. Funny how in less than a month she had memorized Hope's schedule yet she couldn't remember what Aimee's was. She wasn't entirely certain Aimee had a schedule. If Aimee did have a schedule, it was a well-kept secret. Or was it that Pamela had never inquired?

What was happening? What did she do to drive the women she loved away? This morning she was intent on getting an answer from Hope. Was it lack of affection? Lack of interest? Lack of support? And why did she always find the lack in herself and not in her lovers? They seldom seemed void of any of those. Her lovers were without reproach. She was the one with the shortcomings. It had taken her fifteen years of failed relationships to figure this out, and still she repeated the process. The cyclical nature of behavior had become her cross to bear. She wished the crucifixion date would arrive so she could get on with it: molt or resurrection. Anything.

She met Hope while she was opening the door. Hope was having a difficult time balancing her overstuffed appointment book and Nicole's after-school backpack. She was unceremoniously smashing Winnie the Pooh's head beneath her arm.

"I think you're suffocating him," Pamela said.

Hope twirled around. "Suffocating who?"

"Winnie the Pooh."

Hope looked down. "Oh my, I am. How wicked."

"Here, let me help you," Pamela said, divesting Hope of the backpack.

"Thank you. Listen, I'm sorry about yesterday."

"No, you were right on target," Pamela replied with lowered eyes.

"Perhaps you weren't ready for target practice," Hope replied.

"No, I wasn't, but I think I had it coming."

"Do you have time for coffee?" Hope asked.

"Sure."

Hope got the store ready to open and made coffee. They sat down.

"Why am I such an asshole?" Pamela asked.

"I don't think you're an asshole."

"You did when we were together."

Hope got them both coffee in an effort to stall.

"If I tell you, will you promise not to get angry?" Hope asked.

"I promise. I'm losing Aimee, and I don't want to. I need your help."

"All right. You tend to be self-centered, emotionally irresponsible, and sometimes you push away when you need to back down and acquiesce whether you think you're right or not."

"I can accept that."

"So what are you going to do about it?"

"I don't know. How could I have won you back?" Pamela asked.

"That's not a fair question."

"It is. Besides Aimee, you're the only person I really loved. My failure started with you. Tell me how to fix it."

"You act like this is a car with a carburetor problem. Love's not like that," Hope counseled.

"What is it like?" Pamela asked.

"I don't know how to explain it. How do you feel when you look at Aimee?"

"I don't know. Like she is Aimee."

"All right. How did you feel when you used to look at me?" Hope asked.

Pamela blushed.

"Well?" Hope prodded.

"Intense passion."

Hope blushed.

"I'm sorry."

"No, don't be. You don't feel that way with Aimee?"

"I thought I did until one day those kind of feelings stopped. Then an empty spot just started growing again, and I tried to fill it with work."

"But you love her?"

"I do, and I don't like the thought of being without her."

"Okay, that's a start. I don't know what to tell you."

"Tell me why you left," Pamela asked, knowing that this was the question she had driven across the country to find out, that this was what the whole summer was about.

"We're not talking about me," Hope replied.

"But we are."

The front door clanged open, and Emerson and Nic came in.

"She forgot her homework in her pack," Emerson said, as Nic rummaged through Winnie.

"Are you coming to the lake with us tomorrow?" Nic asked Pamela.

"I didn't know you were going."

"We decided this morning. It's Emerson's job to invite everyone," Nic said, looking at Emerson like she was slacking.

"Can Aimee come?" Pamela teased.

"Well, of course," Nic said.

"Is it okay?" Pamela said, looking at Hope.

"Please. I didn't know about it until just now myself," Hope said.

"Okay, off you go," Emerson said, pushing Nic toward the door. "I can only pacify Mrs. Grafton so many times about your tardiness.

"I should go too," Pamela said, getting up abruptly.

"You don't have to," Hope said.

Two customers came in.

"It's getting busy. I'll see you later," Pamela said.

"Okay," Hope said.

Four

Lauren picked up the piece of paper with Aimee's number on it. Friends can call friends. It is not an unusual thing, she thought to herself, so why was she making it difficult? Because you are telling yourself lies, her conscience replied. But why? Because you have ulterior motives. You're infatuated and she's in love with someone else and this is extremely dangerous for your fragile, delicate heart. She put the number down.

Reason stepped in to say she was setting herself up for a fall as well as putting another woman in a compromising position. A suggestive compromising position came to mind. She knew she shouldn't think in those terms, but it was difficult not to. Aimee was the first woman in a long time to make her feel that way. Thinking in sexual terms made her think of love, and love made her think of Jill, and Jill made her think of how much she liked Aimee, because Jill would have liked Aimee and she wouldn't have thought it bad to have a friend. So why was this so hard?

The phone rang and she jumped. It was Emerson.

"Hey, we're all going to the lake tomorrow, and we want you to come. Short notice, but you could drive up in the morning."

"It sounds fun," Lauren replied, not allowing herself to ask if Aimee was going.

"So you're in?"

"Yes."

"Can you do me a favor?"

"Sure."

"Will you call Aimee and see if she wants to go? I've got to get ahold of Berlin and Katherine."

"Okay," Lauren said, feeling her heart leap into her throat.

"You don't mind, do you?"

"No, not at all," Lauren responded, attempting nonchalance.

"It'll give you an excuse to talk to her," Emerson said.

"What's that supposed to mean?" Lauren said, sounding defensive.

"That you like her."

"She's got a girlfriend who is most likely coming to this picnic."

"A girlfriend who treats her like shit. You'd treat her nice."

"You're way out line," Lauren said.

"Which means I'm close to home."

"One more cliché and I'll puke."

"Call and be charming," Emerson suggested.

"I'll try."

Emerson hung up the phone and chugged down half a bottle of Pepto-Bismol.

Pamela walked in the front door to find Aimee on the phone, laughing and highly colored.

"What are you doing?" she asked, obviously annoyed.

"Making potato salad," Aimee replied.

"Not your usual fare," Pamela replied.

"Lauren is coaching me."

"So do you think you got it?" Lauren said, knowing that Pamela had arrived.

"I do. Thank you. Thanks for the invite and for calling," Aimee said, feeling Pamela's hot gaze on her and feeling Lauren's voice wrapping around her as she said good-bye.

"I'll see you tomorrow."

"Yes," Aimee said, turning away from Pamela and holding the phone a moment longer than was necessary.

"Are you in trouble?"

"I could be."

"Shouldn't I have called?" Lauren asked.

"No, I'm glad you did, very glad. No worries, okay?"

Aimee hung up. Pamela was making coffee.

"So where are you going tomorrow?"

"The same place you're going, to the lake. I'm excited. This is going to be fun," Aimee said, still sparkling.

"Why did Lauren call you?" Pamela asked.

"Are you jealous?" Aimee asked.

"No, you would never cheat."

"How can you be so sure?" Aimee replied, suddenly angry with Pamela's certainty.

"Because you're not like that."

"You're right. I'm not," Aimee said, whisking by with the potato salad in hand. She kissed Pamela on the cheek. Pamela grabbed her.

"Where are you going?" she said, pulling Aimee tighter.

"To take the salad to Hope's. I told Nic I'd stop by to see her new paintings.

"You like her, don't you?"

"Lauren?"

"I was referring to Nic," Pamela replied.

Aimee blushed. "I like them both. I miss having friends. You know how I am."

"Yes, the social butterfly."

"Do you mind?" Aimee asked.

"Sometimes. I miss you."

"You're always so busy," Aimee said.

"I could be less busy," Pamela said, kissing her. She saw color rise in Aimee's face.

"I'll be home early," Aimee said.

"I'll be waiting," Pamela said, letting her go.

Aimee walked across town in the fading afternoon light feeling confused, like parts of her were seeping out, leaving smudges behind, testimony to where she had been and where she was going. Lauren made her feel happy to have someone to talk to, and Pamela elicited strong feelings of passion. It was like she needed the two of them rolled up into one. She knew she could feel things for Lauren but she didn't let herself. Lauren needed someone stable and sane, not a quirky English teacher with a bad track record. She sighed, thinking maybe getting laid would make her feel better. She remembered the school psychologist telling her that she often mistook sex for love and that until she learned the difference her relationships would leave a lot to be desired.

When she got to Hope and Emerson's, the door was open and the screen unlatched. She heard voices, but no one responded to her knock. She went in and followed the voices to the bathroom.

Nic was sitting on the toilet with a cloth on her face while Hope held her and asked if she was all right.

"What happened?" Aimee asked.

Nic took the cloth off to reveal her black eye.

"How did you get that?" Aimee asked, instantly concerned.

"It's a hate crime, that's how she got it," Camille said. She had come right over when she heard about Nic's altercation at school. She'd beaten Berlin getting there, which left Berlin fuming. Hope couldn't be so impolite as to not let her in. Katherine was trying to control Berlin, but so far it wasn't working.

"It is not a hate crime," Berlin said adamantly. "Why do you blow everything out of proportion like this? You should go back to California where they need people like you."

"California has enough people like me. It's these small bastions of lesbians that need me," Camille declared.

"We don't need you. We need peace and quiet, not a bunch of stirred up townspeople," Berlin replied hotly.

"Berlin, I took you for a mover and shaker, not a coward," Camille said.

Katherine grabbed Berlin's arm. "I am not a coward. You're a meddler."

"That's what they call all activists," Camille retorted.

Berlin took a deep breath and made a hasty exit. "You bug me."

"That was pretty tame," Hope whispered to Katherine.

"She didn't get her afternoon nap."

"I thought you might be changing her," Hope replied.

"Never. Not even old age will do that," Katherine said.

"So how did you get the black eye?" Aimee asked.

"I got into a fight with Johnnie Miller. I punched him in the mouth," Nic said.

"What started it?" Aimee asked, sitting on the edge of the tub and giving Nic her full attention.

"He called my moms rug munchers," Nic replied sheepishly.

Aimee burst out laughing. Camille scowled at her.

"This is a serious matter, young lady," Camille reprimanded.

"I'm sorry," Aimee said, trying to compose herself.

Hope smiled at her. "It's all right. We thought it was pretty funny too, but Nic obviously took offense.

"It's not a nice thing to say. I didn't call his mother a cocksucker. Same difference."

"Nic!"

"Sorry, Mom. Can I go now? I want to show Aimee my paintings. My eye feels better. Honest," Nic said, trying to extricate herself from a bathroom full of women.

Hope took the potato salad from Aimee.

When Aimee got back from the viewing, Camille had left. Hope handed her a glass of wine.

"That woman drives me to drink," Berlin said, refilling her glass.

"What's her deal?" Aimee asked.

"She doesn't think the town is gay enough, basically," Emerson responded.

"No, not lesbian enough. She doesn't even want men in her town," Katherine replied.

"It's not her town!" Berlin screeched.

"Well, she's looking to be mayor," Katherine said.

"Over my dead body," Berlin muttered, pouring everyone more wine and emptying the bottle. "Do you have any more of this?"

Emerson pulled another bottle off the rack.

Berlin examined it. "Good year."

Aimee helped Hope put Nic to bed. It was nice tucking her in with her bears and blankets and eyes growing sleepy.

"You like kids, don't you?" Hope asked, as they walked down the stairs.

"I think kids like me."

"Ever think about having one?"

"Only if they were like Nic," Aimee said, smiling.

"How did Pamela end up with such a charming woman?"

"An accident, I assure you," Aimee replied, attempting to be lightly sardonic.

"Is everything okay?" Hope asked.

103

"I don't know."

"We can talk if you'd ever want to," Hope offered.

"I know, and I appreciate it. I just don't have the words yet. Does that make sense?"

"Perfect sense," Hope said, touching Aimee's shoulder.

When they got back downstairs the cigar smoking Scrabble game had begun. "Want to play?" Berlin asked, handing Aimee a cigar.

"I don't smoke cigars," Aimee said.

"You do now," Berlin said, lighting it for her.

Emerson scooted over, and Aimee sat down.

"So here's the rules. Tonight it's lesbian Scrabble," Berlin said with a mischievous glint in her eye.

"Lesbian Scrabble!" Katherine said, busily arranging her letters and then passing the box to Aimee.

"It's in honor of Camille. We start with Scrabble, then we move on to bigger ideas," Berlin stated. "I'll show her just how lesbian we can be."

"In any language? And can we use proper names?" Aimee asked.

"Of course," Berlin replied, eyeing Aimee as obvious competition.

The game began with the easy words coming up first.

"I think I need a little help in terms of definitions. It means anything pertaining to lesbians — lifestyle, behavior, code words, et cetera?" Hope asked.

"Yes," Berlin replied, refilling Aimee's glass.

"I hate Scrabble," Emerson whined.

"That's just because you're not good at it," Berlin replied.

"Words are not my forte," Emerson grumbled, putting down her letters.

"C-o-m-e," Emerson spelled out.

"Gee, that's original," Berlin taunted.

"It's what I do best," Emerson retorted.

Aimee smiled wickedly at Katherine and Berlin. She put

down an odd assortment of letters that made absolutely no sense.

"What is that?" Berlin replied, indignantly.

"It's Sanskrit for muff diving," Aimee replied, calculating her points.

"What!" Berlin screeched.

"You said any language," Aimee replied.

"She's right. You did say that," Katherine said.

"We can't possibly check it. Like I have a Sanskrit dictionary," Berlin replied.

"Exactly," Aimee replied.

"Okay, then here's my word," Hope replied, putting down another equally obscure word. "It's goddess language for nipple sucking."

"This is totally outrageous," Berlin complained.

"No, this is unconventional and inventive," Katherine replied. "And it is something that Camille in all her purity would not condone."

Berlin raised an eyebrow. "I might be able to abide by that. All right. If you can come up with a viable word, it will be accepted."

"Does everyone agree?" Hope asked.

The consensus was for inventing, although Berlin said the new game rules were highly irregular.

"Since when have you been regular?" Emerson chided.

"I have my moments," Berlin retorted.

It wasn't until Berlin deposited Aimee on her front porch that she had time to decipher the evening. All Aimee really knew for certain was the warm feeling of belonging that lingered in her drunken brain, that these women wanted to know her for who she was at this moment in time and no other reason.

Berlin gave her a hug and gently pushed her toward the front door.

"So I get a rematch tomorrow right?" Aimee asked.

"You most certainly do. I finally have some competition. I expect you will sharpen my skills. Now you get inside before that beautiful wife of yours throws you out for being naughty. You tell her it was all my fault."

Aimee smiled. If the light had been better and they had drunk less, Berlin would have caught the sadness in Aimee's eyes. Then she remembered her question.

"Berlin, do you know what happened in this house? Where the O'Malleys went?" Aimee asked.

"They went away," Berlin hedged.

"Obviously," Aimee said. "It's a mystery that I'd like to solve. Either no one knows or the ones who know won't tell. Come on," Aimee prodded.

"O'Malley's wife was a diabetic, had been most her life. Kept to herself a lot, so no one really knew much about her until one day she died. The doctors said it was inevitable, but the lady next door who used to come in and check on her said the old man did her in. Didn't keep up on her medication or her diet. She said O'Malley did it on purpose to collect the insurance money. As soon as she was buried he left town, left the house, didn't take anything but his clothes," Berlin said.

"So it's a nasty little town secret," Aimee said.

"I guess so. It's hard to say if he really did it or not," Berlin said.

"Maybe that's how straight people left each other in those days," Aimee said, trying to lighten up the mood.

"That's how Camille would look at it."

"What are you going to do if she runs for mayor?" Aimee asked.

"You and I are going to sabotage her campaign," Berlin said.

106

"Why me?"

"Because you're tricky and you're smart. You're also a lot more spry than I am. Deal?"

"Sure."

"I'll see you later," Berlin said.

Aimee sat down on the porch and watched Berlin amble up the street, smoking a cigar and acting like the world was her infinite playground. Aimee found it odd that women felt safe here, but Berlin had told her that the town had a way of taking care of its own. If a man hurt a woman they wouldn't wait for legal justice, they'd cut his balls off right there and then. Swift justice, Berlin called it, and it kept people in line. We're accountable here, and it makes a difference. Berlin didn't believe in big-city life. Towns have community, cities have anonymity. She was right. Aimee often felt lost in that sea of faces where most behavior had little consequence.

Yet even in this small town she felt lost. I just want to matter, she told herself. Matter like the women of the town mattered to each other, the way they had a past and future with each other rather than an endless stream of people going through their lives with no real substance, with no sense of connection, spending time, but not weaving the cords of their lives together. Not even as lovers did she feel that same kind of connection with Pamela. Not the way Hope looked at Emerson or Katherine at Berlin.

For all the laughter, chiding, and jokes that night, Aimee felt sad, the endless outsider. Maybe that was how her father felt, the resident alien, a citizen but never a countryman, and that was why he threw himself into his work and away from people. I don't want to do that, Aimee told herself. I want to live and laugh and share things. She started to cry, thinking her wish an impossibility. She knew at the end of the summer she would go back to the city and work and try to forget what life could be like. The realization hit her hard. Big truths are the hardest to stomach, and she felt like she was trying to swallow a boulder.

Pamela found her sobbing on the front porch. She touched her shoulder. Aimee looked up and saw Pamela standing there looking puzzled, her long hair loose about her shoulders, dressed only in a long T-shirt.

"Aimee, what's wrong?"

"Nothing. Just a bad moment. I'm okay," Aimee said, trying to quickly compose herself.

"What happened tonight? What did they do to you?" Pamela asked.

"Nothing. We played Scrabble. I was just thinking about things. I'm okay, really. Let's go inside."

Pamela held her for a moment and felt her shaking. "I missed you tonight," she whispered.

Aimee started to cry again, feeling guilty for not feeling the same, for holding Pamela responsible for part of her own emptiness.

"Come on. It's okay. Let's go to bed. You smell like cigars."

Aimee laughed. "Berlin got me smoking them."

Pamela smiled. "That's better," she said, as she pulled Aimee's T-shirt off and helped her get into bed. She rolled in next to Aimee and held her, stroking her face.

"Are you sure you don't want to talk about it?"

"Yeah, I'm just tired," Aimee said, nestling in close.

Pamela stroked her neck and then her breast, moving her hand down Aimee's back, thinking of earlier when Aimee had promised to make love, thinking now would be a good time, would make Aimee feel better. Aimee moved away.

"No, please. I can't right now," Aimee said, and started to cry again.

"Okay," Pamela said, reaching for the tissue on the nightstand.

~ ~ ~ ~ ~

Aimee was quiet and hung over in the morning. Pamela did her best not to be irritable. She hadn't slept well last night. The stress of the two sets of neuroses, her own and whatever was going on with Aimee was starting to wear her patience thin. All she had wanted was to spend a quiet night at home with Aimee. Instead she got left for the evening, both physically and emotionally. Pamela supposed it was her own fault as she had done the same thing to Aimee countless times.

"Are you better?" Pamela asked, as she made her way straight for the coffeemaker.

Aimee poured her a cup.

"Yes. I'm sorry about last night. Too much to drink."

"They do drink a lot here," Pamela said, going out to get the paper. Coffee, cigarettes, and the written word would give her back her sense of sanity and order. She sat out on the front porch while Aimee took a shower. She half thought about joining her, but last night's rebuke sat uneasily in the back of her mind. She wasn't in the mood for another rejection.

The road up to Fisk Lake was windy but pretty in its pristinely lined edges. Aimee saw only flashes of green as she held her head out the window, trying to get some air. Emerson and Hope had put her up front with them in the old pickup truck in an effort to keep Aimee from puking. She didn't look good. Berlin was highly sympathetic because she also didn't feel good. Lauren looked on with concern, while Pamela was obviously not amused.

"It's entirely my fault," Berlin said. "It may have been the cigars."

Pamela nodded tersely. "We probably should have stayed home."

"I'll feel better after lunch," Aimee said, grabbing a blanket and scouting around for the nearest tree.

"I'm coming with you," Berlin said.

Aimee lay down on a blanket with Berlin where she took a short nap until lunch.

"I don't want to get hangovers when I grow up," Nic said.

"That's a good thing," Hope replied, putting sunscreen on Nic's shoulders.

Aimee watched the strings of woven clouds drifting by and the sun sparkling across the surface of the lake like tiny pieces of glass. She could hear the sounds of the picnic party and she lay thinking of how pretty it was here with the big oak trees and the warm smell of grass and earth and how she should be happy in such a nice place. Lately, the only time she felt good was in Lauren's presence. Now she was busy screwing that up as she lay sick, wondering what would Lauren think of her. She felt awful and sad, knowing that what Lauren probably saw was a woman with a drinking problem who chose bitches for girlfriends. That looked good. Aimee was beginning to realize that she spent a lot of time thinking about Lauren, and that made her feel worse. She knew she was in no position to have those feelings. She closed her eyes and concentrated on Berlin's even breathing.

Lauren helped Hope and Katherine get the picnic set up. She stole glances at Aimee who was sleeping soundly.

"All right. Go get the sleeping beauties, Nic, and be gentle," Hope said. She sneaked over and gently kissed each on the cheek. Lauren watched Aimee regain consciousness before she went over to help her up.

"Feeling better?" Lauren asked, extending her hand.

"A little. I think food will help," Aimee replied, taking Lauren's hand.

"I know food will help," Berlin said, rubbing her eyes and

surveying the picnic spread. "Let's go," she said, hopping up spryly for a woman in her sixties.

Aimee ate carefully. Berlin ate like a horse and went back for seconds. After lunch they all spread out on the selection of blankets to rest.

Hope turned to Aimee. "I forgot to tell you that the triplets called the store this morning. They said, or rather Honour said, she had misplaced your number but remembered you telling them about the bookstore. I thought that was neat," Hope said.

"The triplets!" Pamela screeched.

"Did I say something wrong?" Hope inquired, looking nervously at Aimee.

"No. When are they coming?" Aimee asked. Please don't let it be today, she thought.

"Soon. They don't have an exact date yet, but they are moving this way."

Berlin, obviously interested, leaned in.

"Triplets? Lesbian triplets?" she asked.

"You didn't tell me they were coming," Pamela said, glaring at Aimee.

"I hadn't quite got around to it," Aimee said.

"I'm sorry," Hope said.

"It's not your fault. Pamela doesn't like them."

"I can't believe you invited them," Pamela said.

"They're my friends, and they're running races that are close by. It's only normal they would stop by here."

"There is absolutely nothing normal about those psychotic women," Pamela said, her voice reaching a high pitch.

"They're not psychotic," Aimee replied.

"I beg to differ," Pamela said, noticing she had an audience. "You tell me if I'm out of line here."

"Do tell," Berlin said.

"Ouch!" Berlin said, rubbing the spot where Katherine had pitched her.

Aimee lay down, groaned, and rolled her eyes.

Lauren gave her a sympathetic look. Nic crawled in closer, sensing it was story time. Aimee winked at Nic.

"The very first time I met these women was at an extremely wild undergraduate party that I'd been forced to attend. One of them had Aimee hanging over a second-story balcony by her ankles while the other two screamed at the one perpetrating the crime to put her down or rather pull her up. She refused, insistent upon extricating a confession from Aimee about whether she was sleeping with the other two sisters.

"I certainly hope you didn't have change in your pockets," Berlin teased.

"I didn't," Aimee replied.

"What does *extricate* mean?" Nic whispered to Aimee.

"Get something out of you," Aimee whispered back.

"Like when I had to tell my mom about crashing on my bike?"

"Exactly," Aimee replied.

Lauren looked over at Aimee, who was showing Nic how to make whistling noises from a blade of thick grass.

"Well, did you?" Berlin asked, raising a lascivious eyebrow.

Katherine rolled her eyes and stated the obvious, "There is no controlling Berlin's curiosity when it comes to anything lesbian."

"Did I what?" Aimee responded.

"Sleep with the triplets?" Berlin prodded.

"No, it was game, a show we used to put on."

"Some game. Honour almost killed you," Pamela said.

"Did she drop you?" Nic asked, her eyes big.

"No," Aimee replied, knowing full well what was coming.

"How did she almost kill you?" Hope asked.

"She shot her with a crossbow," Pamela said flatly.

"Do we have to go into the crossbow thing or, as the dean of students referred to it, the heretofore Crossbow Incident?" Aimee replied stoically.

"Did it hurt?" Nic asked.

"A little."

"Show them your arm," Pamela demanded.

"No!"

Nic searched Aimee's arms until she found the scar. "Here it is," she proudly exclaimed.

"See, it's not that bad," Aimee said, pulling her sleeve up. Several pairs of eyes leaned over.

"Why did she do that?" Berlin asked.

"We were playing William Tell in the backyard during a party. It was a routine, like the balcony thing. We were just messing around. Honour would demand I confess to sleeping with Hannah and Holly, and I'd refuse and she would put me to the test. Only this time some zealot attempted to save me. She tried to get the crossbow away from Honour, and the arrow came flying out," Aimee said, replaying the scene in her head.

The thrust of the arrow was intense as it struck her arm. She fell to the ground. The look of horror on the triplets' faces made her wonder for a brief second if her arm was detached. She touched it gently. She felt the warm ooze of blood. Then an argument ensued over whether they should remove the arrow or leave it in and take her to emergency. The group of people standing around inspecting her arm was making her increasingly sick until she backed away, arrow still rooted, and puked. Hannah took control, and they drove her to the hospital. The admitting clerk was already stressed with a slew of other weekend accidents. She didn't even look up while she asked the nature of the problem.

"She's got a goddamn arrow sticking out of her arm, you fucking moron," Honour screamed.

"Now, that's enough, young lady," the matronly nurse replied. She looked up at Aimee, and her eyes got large.

"Oh my," she said and took Aimee, who was now quite

thoroughly drenched in blood, back to a treatment room. Due to the nature of the wound, the police were called. When it came time to charge someone, the triplets all confessed, which sent the red-faced police officer into fits. It was difficult to get a statement because the witnesses couldn't honestly tell which triplet had shot the arrow. As the doctor removed the arrow, Aimee kept insisting it was an accident and that no one should be charged with anything.

The dean of students was notified because the incident had taken place on school property and involved students. The triplets' mother was horrified. And since they stuck together, the dean was forced to throw them all out of school.

Aimee's father had come to see her, or, rather, the nature of her wound. They'd kept her at the hospital for a few days because the doctors were worried about her arm. It had been a serious wound, and Aimee would spend months in physical therapy to repair the damage. She was relieved the triplets were at Berkeley so they didn't have to see the aftermath of that rather fateful day.

That day marked the beginning of growing up, of understanding the fine line between adventurous free spirit and derangement. Aimee's father sat down heavily in the chair by her bed, which always fascinated Aimee that a man of so slight a frame could sit down so heavily, with such an immense force as to practically supplant the very air in the room. He held his hat in his lap. She studied his thin wrists as they folded themselves neatly over his hat.

She still found it odd that he wore a hat when men no longer wore them, another indication that he was not part of this new world, which further made him an anomaly because as an engineer he built new worlds. Staring at him that day she realized that it was from such confusion of thought, action, and philosophy that she had come. Was it any wonder she was such a mess? Her mother was in Spain using travel as a way to avoid her father without the disgrace of divorce.

She used postcards and credit-card bills as a means of communication.

"I have only a few things to say to you," he began. "I don't pretend to understand what makes you seek women as lovers and I have no desire to, but I ask you to choose them with more discretion and not to choose people who will hurt —"

"But it was an accident —"

"Listen to me. I am simply asking that in the future you choose your lovers more wisely, with more discretion, and that you learn to harness your desire into something positive. I want you to finish school and enter the professions. It is simple. Do not disappoint me," he said, getting up and leaving before Aimee had a chance to say anything else.

She honored his wishes, not because he asked her to but because suddenly she understood that he was telling her his own story. Love would ruin her if she let it. Love would keep her from herself. It would bind her tighter, hold her down longer, and crush her with more malice than any drug, any unjust regime, any illness of mind or body ever could. Love could be the most destructive weapon on the face of the heart's landscape, and, more often than not, love is in the hands of fools.

"She could have killed you," Lauren said, snapping Aimee back from her memories.

"I know. But she hadn't meant to, and the dean did throw them out of school."

"Thank goodness for that. Who knows what would have happened had you and Honour continued to be lovers," Pamela said.

"Well, the crossbow incident certainly put an end to that," Aimee said, remembering the look on Honour's face when she found out Aimee wasn't going with them to Berkeley. Honour saw it as complete betrayal and had then proceeded to throw every plate, bowl, and glass, across the kitchen at her while she screamed a litany of obscenities. Aimee fled when she had the chance, ended up crying in Hannah's arms, trying to explain herself.

"So now, you tell me if you think they're certifiably insane," Pamela said, looking at her audience.

"Perhaps a little rambunctious," Hope said diplomatically.

"That's putting it mildly. Anyway, I don't want them coming," Pamela said.

"They're my friends, and they're coming," Aimee said.

"Why do you want to be around someone that hurt you like that?" Pamela demanded.

"It was an accident."

"Not that," Pamela said, impatiently.

"I hurt her too." Here goes round two, Aimee thought.

"Why, because you grew up and she didn't?" Pamela taunted.

"She's my friend, they're my friends, and I miss them."

"Honour is still madly in love with you. God knows why after all that happened. Together you all get psychotic, and I can't begin to concentrate in such an environment," Pamela stated.

"At least someone is still madly in love with me," Aimee countered.

"What's that supposed to mean?" Pamela said, glaring.

"Think about it. Nic, let's go make a sand castle so I can blow it up when we're done," Aimee said, getting up abruptly.

"Yeah!" Nic said, following behind her.

~ ~ ~ ~ ~

"Okay, now looks like a good time to start that game of Scrabble," Berlin said.

"Good idea," Katherine said, pulling the board game from her immense duffel bag.

"Are you in?" Emerson asked Lauren.

"No, I'll watch," Lauren replied.

Pamela had dived into her page proofs, making it apparent she didn't have time for board games.

"This isn't going to be nearly so much fun without Aimee," Berlin pined, giving Pamela a dirty look.

"Be nice," Katherine warned.

"Well, it isn't," Berlin muttered.

During a break while Berlin was seriously contemplating her letters, intent on making a big move, Emerson got three sodas from the ice chest and the suntan lotion.

Lauren looked up inquiringly as Emerson plopped them down in front of her. "Thirsty?"

"Her shoulders are getting burned and I'm sure they are both thirsty. Go, it's where you want to be."

Lauren glanced over at Pamela.

"She won't even notice. I guarantee it."

Lauren smiled appreciatively at Emerson.

Aimee looked up at Lauren.

"You two thirsty?" she asked.

"Parched," Aimee said, wiping her sandy hands on her cutoffs and taking the soda.

"I would have brought you a beer but —" Lauren said.

"No, soda is better."

"You're burning."

Aimee looked at her shoulders, which were turning pink. "You're right. I forgot sunscreen."

117

"I just happen to have some," Lauren said, sitting down behind Aimee.

"Why do you like Honour when she hurt you like that?" Nic asked.

"Let me tell you the story of the grapefruit and the apricot."

"Okay," Nic said, scooping up more sand and forming it with a plastic cup.

"See, they used to be together every day in the lunch box, and every day the grapefruit would roll back and forth and bruise the apricot, but the apricot loved the grapefruit and the grapefruit loved the apricot. The grapefruit didn't mean to hurt the apricot, but because she was bigger and tougher, when she rolled against the apricot it would hurt her. But the apricot didn't mind because she knew the grapefruit loved her. So together they would be lunch, knowing that it was all right because what was soft was not bad, nor was what was hard, only different."

"Oh, I get it."

"Good," Aimee said smiling.

"That was nice," Lauren said, rubbing Aimee's back with sunscreen, across her shoulders and down her back, careful to not go too close to her breasts yet beneath her armpits. Aimee squirmed a little. Nic's face lit up. Lauren moved her hand there again just to make sure.

"Nic, I've found a rare commodity," Lauren said.

"She's ticklish!" Nic said, inching closer.

"We don't have many ticklish people in these parts do we Nic?"

"No, we don't."

"All right I admit to being slightly ticklish," Aimee said, not getting any sensation that she was about to be attacked.

Lauren started in from behind while Nic went for her feet and tummy. Aimee screamed and then tried to squirm away while Lauren and Nic were in fits of laughter. Even Pamela looked up for a brief moment.

118

"C'mon, you guys. That's enough really . . . I mean it. Stop or I'll —"

Nic jumped up first. "She threw up."

Lauren was mortified.

Aimee sat up.

"I'm so sorry. Maybe I just thought I was better."

"We shouldn't have moved you around so much. Come into the water. It'll make you feel better," Lauren said, taking Aimee's hands and pulling her into the lake.

Aimee could see Nic relaying information and Pamela's look of disgust.

"Let me take you home," Lauren said, getting Aimee a towel and wrapping it around her shoulders.

"I think I'd better," Aimee replied.

"She doesn't feel well," Lauren explained to the anxious onlookers. "I'll take her home, if that's all right."

"I think that's a good idea. We can bring Pamela home later. If that's all right," Hope said, looking at Pamela.

"Fine," Pamela said.

Lauren sighed with inward relief as she helped Aimee to the car.

Aimee leaned out the window most of the way home while Lauren drove, anxious and quiet.

Aimee finally sat back into the seat and looked over at Lauren.

"I'm sorry I ruined your picnic."

"I only went to the picnic to see you," Lauren said, swallowing hard.

Aimee smiled and brushed a stray hair from Lauren's face.

"Me too," Aimee said.

"So do you really want to go home? Or could I entice you into being a couch potato and watching a movie?" Lauren asked.

"Sounds wonderful."

"Do you like Peter Greenaway?"

Aimee sat up immediately. "Do you?"

"I can't believe I found someone who even knows who he is," Lauren said.

"He's my favorite. Can we watch *Murder by Numbers* or *Zoo* but not *The Cook*, for obvious reasons?"

"Yes, that is perfectly understandable. Let's watch them both. Then we don't have to decide. I don't, however, want to get you in trouble," Lauren said, looking at her watch. It was still early.

"Getting drunk last night and puking got me in trouble. I'll be all right."

They stopped by the grocery store and then the video store, grabbing all the necessary provisions. Aimee was taxed by the time they got to Lauren's loft apartment. Nausea had returned, and she felt cold and clammy.

"Let me run a bath and get you some dry clothes," Lauren said.

"I think I need to lie down for a minute," Aimee said, sitting back on the couch.

Lauren started the bath and then fluttered about the loft getting everything set up just right for watching the movie.

"Okay, the bath's ready," Lauren said.

Aimee crept toward the bathroom.

The bathwater felt good as she eased into it. Lauren knocked on the door with clothes and a glass of soda.

"Are you decent?"

"As a rule, no," Aimee teased. "But I am covered with bubbles if you want to come in."

Lauren opened the door tentatively and stuck her head in.

"What? You don't believe me?" Aimee chided.

"I do," Lauren said blushing.

The color had come back in Aimee's face.

"I commend you on your good taste in bath accessories. Of course, everything about you is extremely tasteful."

"Is that bad?" Lauren asked, immediately alarmed.

"No, it's lovely," Aimee said, taking the soda from Lauren. "Hopefully, this will settle your stomach, and if we don't move you around anymore, you'll feel better," Lauren ventured.

"I'm sure with you playing nurse I'd be miraculously cured," Aimee replied.

Lauren smiled and left.

Aimee ran her big toe along the smooth chrome faucet and thought about things she shouldn't be thinking about.

Lauren put the popcorn in the microwave and thanked the stars above for hangovers, for without them she would not have been given this afternoon alone with Aimee. Maybe the universe was finally doing her a favor. She pretended for an indulgent half-second that she and Aimee were hanging out together, that she wasn't borrowing someone else's girlfriend, that this friendship would go other places, better, warmer, closer places. She lay back on the bed and closed her eyes, listening to the noises from the bathroom, imagining Aimee's naked body in the warm water, her smooth curves, the long plane of her back, the gentle swoop between her ribs and hips.

The sunshine danced through the open window and across the wood floor while the breeze blew the white curtain back and forth slowly. Lauren watched its movement, becoming hypnotized by the regularity. She closed her eyes and thought of Aimee, Aimee in her arms. How soft and small she would be and how hungry Lauren felt wanting to touch in those special places reserved only for lovers. She didn't care that Aimee had a past. She cared only that she might want a future with someone other than Pamela. With this sacrilegious prayer on her lips, Lauren dozed off.

Aimee got out of the tub and found Lauren asleep on the bed. She sat down quietly and studied Lauren, thinking of the beautiful serenity of her face when she slept. The way a parent gazes upon her child and a lover upon her beloved, able to capture for a moment angelic peace, perfect calm, and the very essence of vulnerability, a kind of brief rapture of the soul.

Then she thought about waking up beside that beautiful woman. How every morning could be the beginning of a day like today, where they cared about each other and could talk and not have animosity, where she could be in love and not feel apologetic for needing things. For the first time in a long time she thought about falling in love. She thought about Lauren until sleep captured her as well.

The groans of the coffeemaker woke Aimee. She wandered toward the kitchen, still rubbing her eyes and trying to orient herself.

She smiled at Lauren. "Well, I guess we got that out of the way."

"What?"

"Sleeping together," Aimee said, taking the proffered cup of coffee.

"I certainly hoped it would have entailed more than napping," Lauren teased back.

Aimee came closer and put her arm around Lauren's shoulder, "Oh yes, it would. It definitely would."

"Good," Lauren said.

"Thanks for taking care of me," Aimee said.

"You're most welcome. Still feel like watching the movie?"

"Of course."

"In here or the other television?"

"You mean the one in the bedroom?" Aimee replied, putting emphasis on bedroom. "I vote bedroom."

"I promise to behave myself," Lauren chided.

"Damn."

They sat on the bed, ate popcorn, drank Coke and dissected the movie, explaining this or that part for the other. It was as if they were longtime companions, laughing and enjoying themselves in that easy way only people who are totally comfortable with one another can obtain. In between movies Lauren asked Aimee about Honour.

"I don't know what happened with us. There was the one little episode after the crossbow and before the triplets left for California that really put an end to our relationship and almost put an end to the sisterhood," Aimee said, thinking of the scratching noise the record player made that day as it went round and round.

"You have to promise not to tell," Aimee said.

"I wouldn't tell."

"Because Pamela would have a heyday if she knew."

"You slept with the triplets . . ." Lauren ventured.

"No."

Lauren breathed easier.

"I slept with Hannah, and Honour found us together in bed. It's not as torrid as it sounds. Honour went berserk when she found out I wasn't going with them to Berkeley and then proceeded to throw every breakable thing in the kitchen at me. I went to see Hannah, we got to talking, and one thing led to another. I guess we both realized we had feelings for each other but Honour got there first, like she always does. In some ways, I think that we were saying hello and good-bye all in the same afternoon. Anyway, it was a mess, and it's amazing we're still friends."

"Wow."

"After Honour and that whole scene, Pamela appeared rather restful. She leaves me alone . . . too much sometimes. So as my mother would say, I've botched up being a lesbian."

"Why do you say that?"

"Because I don't make a very good one."

"What do you mean? You're a lesbian's dream. You're witty, beautiful, smart, successful, and you have an incredible body," Lauren said, her face going instantly red.

"I like you, too. You do wonders for my crumbling self

esteem. You're not so bad yourself, you know," Aimee said, cocking her head to one side and squeezing Lauren's outstretched hand. "So tell me. Why do I choose such lousy lovers?"

"You haven't found the right one."

"Good answer."

On the way back from the lake Nic begged to ride in the back of the old pickup. Hope agreed only if she supervised. The wind blew their hair around, and the setting sun gave the running landscape the soft light Hope loved best. The glare of the day done, she could sink slowly into night in relaxed contentment. Her daughter smiled up at her and snuggled closer, picking up on her mother's mood.

"Mom?"

"Yes, Nic?"

"Why did Lauren take care of Aimee when she was sick instead of Pamela?"

"I don't know, Nic. Some people are just better at things like that. Maybe Lauren felt bad for making Aimee throw up."

"I think Aunt Lauren likes Aimee."

"I'm sure she does."

"Really likes her."

"What are trying to say, Nic?"

"I think she loves her."

"Are you jealous?" Hope asked.

"Kind of, but I want Aunt Lauren to be happy, and Aimee makes her smile."

"So you're willing to give her up?"

"Well, yes, but what will happen with . . . you know," Nic whispered, pointing to the cab of the truck where Pamela was sitting in awkward silence with Emerson. The radio was broken so there was nothing to do but listen to the whir of the tires on the highway.

"I don't know, Nic," Hope replied.

Nic nodded and then closed her eyes and took a nap.

They dropped Pamela off at her house. The house was dark, and the early evening glow had descended into the dark of night. Pamela waved good-bye from the porch while Nic and Hope crept in front with Emerson.

"Boy was that fun or what," Emerson said, rolling her eyes. "I hope you appreciate that, young lady."

"I do. Thank you," Nic said, taking Emerson's hand. "I just needed to talk to Mom."

"Okay, you're forgiven."

There were no lights on in the house, and Pamela thought Aimee must be sleeping off her hangover. She wasn't angry with her anymore. The afternoon at the lake had turned out much better than she'd expected. It was nice spending the day with Hope. Pamela had forgotten what an amiable listener Hope was, and Pamela had spent the day telling Hope about the book project and her hopes for the future. She felt sure she saw pride shining in Hope's eyes, and that made her happy.

Pamela made her way quietly to the bedroom and gently opened the door, expecting to find her Aimee asleep. The bed was empty. It didn't look like Aimee had been home at all. A hard lump formed in her stomach. She'd been had. Her wife had absconded with Lauren, and lord knew where they were. Pamela checked the answering machine, only to find a message from Honour. She clicked it off in rage, calling Honour a cunt under her breath.

She poured herself a drink and sat down to wait. She felt her rage beginning to take form. She picked up a book and tried to read, but all she could see was Lauren wrapping a towel around Aimee's shoulders and announcing that she was taking her home. And now Honour was coming to town.

Aimee and Pamela were supposed to be spending the summer getting together, but instead it seemed she and Aimee were drifting farther apart. She heard a car pull up out front. She pretended to read, but her heart was pumping fast. It was the next-door neighbors. She poured another drink.

Emerson wrapped her arms around Hope in the kitchen while they listened to messages left from the day. The last one was from Pamela asking Hope to call her in the morning.

"Was she always such a cold fish?" Emerson asked.

Hope smiled, "Yes, darling," as she slipped her hand up Emerson's shirt until it rested rather boldly on her nipple.

"Did you find me overwhelming at first after hanging around with her?"

"In comparison?" Hope asked, kissing Emerson's neck.

"Yes."

"No, I found you to be a wonderful contrast that I couldn't help falling in love with," Hope replied.

"Is that what Aimee might be feeling?" Emerson queried. She was still learning about reading other people's impulses. Hope was working on making her less self-involved. But reading other people's intentions always troubled Emerson. She depended on Hope to be her emotional thermometer.

"Would you be surprised?"

"No."

"Me either," Hope replied, running her hand down the front of Emerson's pants. Finding her wet, she slipped her fingers inside.

"What will you do if it happens?" Emerson asked, going up the back of Hope's shirt and feeling her smooth skin as she pulled her closer.

"Pick up the pieces, send Pamela on her way, and adopt Aimee into the family."

"Really?" Emerson asked, surprised.

"Enough talk. Take me to bed this instant."

"Can we walk like this?" Emerson inquired, willing to give it a valiant effort.

"Let's try," Hope suggested.

The blue screen cut across the room. Aimee and Lauren sat propped up on pillows on the bed talking. Lauren looked across the room. The clock said ten-thirty. She had offered to take Aimee home earlier, but to no avail.

"I should take you home. It's late."

"I know, but I've had such fun."

"Me too."

The town was dark and quiet as they drove across it.

"You're a night owl, aren't you?"

"How did you guess," Aimee said, smiling. "It's quiet and so peaceful."

"Yes, it is," Lauren replied, looking up at the stars as they waited for the light to change. They were in no hurry. Lauren drove slowly. They pulled up in front of the house. Lauren got out to open the trunk and retrieve Aimee's backpack.

"I have to stay in Santa Fe this week," Lauren said, shyly.

"Life will be quite dull without you," Aimee said, taking Lauren's hand, letting her cool fingers slip into Lauren's hand.

"Emerson is coming down to help me with the philanthropists. If you want you could come down . . . if you could manage it," Lauren said.

Aimee smiled. "I'd love to."

"Wonderful. I'll arrange it with Emerson. I'd really like to see you."

"How many days do I have to wait?"

"Just until Wednesday," Lauren replied.

"It'll be hard, but I think I can last that long," Aimee teased, knowing she was flirting but not caring to restrain herself.

Aimee opened the front door quietly. Pamela sat on the couch waiting.

"Have a nice time?" she jeered.

"Yes. Sorry I'm late. We watched movies."

"As in plural?"

"Yes," Aimee said, surveying the half-empty bottle of scotch. She felt her heart quicken and her mouth get dry. "I should have called," she said, trying to pacify. She was tired and didn't want a scene.

"Are you sleeping with her?"

"No!" Aimee replied, with enough indignation to make it read true.

"But that doesn't mean you don't want to."

"It's not like that," Aimee replied, realizing that what she felt for Lauren wasn't about lust or infatuation or the newness of curiosity. It was something far deeper, something touching on precious.

"What's it like then?" Pamela said, coming closer, cornering Aimee between the wall and the kitchen archway.

"I don't know. We're friends."

"Friends that are falling in love," Pamela said, inching closer.

"Don't go there."

"Where would you like me to go?"

"I just want to go bed. I'm tired. Please," Aimee pleaded.

"I bet. I thought you were sick. Or was that simply a ploy to get the two of you alone?"

"No. I was sick and she took care of me, which was more than you were offering," Aimee said, trying to make a dash for the kitchen.

Pamela grabbed and pinned her against the wall.

"Where the fuck do you think you're going?"

"Let me go," Aimee said, trying not to panic.

"Not until you tell me the truth."

"I told you the truth. We're friends. We're not fucking or any of those other euphemisms you have for love."

"Tell me the truth!" Pamela screamed, pinching Aimee's arms and slamming her harder against the wall.

Aimee felt her feet leave the floor, and she tried hard not to cry. She thought of her mother's rages and how crying only made it worse. The pain in her arms grew greater until she couldn't stop the tears.

"What are you crying for? You're the one fucking everything up. You're getting what you want. A way to punish me for whatever it is I've done to you. Stop crying. That's not going to help. I didn't bring you here to lose you to someone else. I'm not going to let that happen again. Do you understand?" Pamela said, holding her tighter.

"You're hurting me," Aimee sobbed.

Pamela let go, then let out a deep sigh, grabbed her cigarettes, and went outside, saying nothing. Aimee slunk to the floor crying.

When Aimee composed herself, she got sheets and blankets for the spare bedroom and locked the door. She tried not to remember other times in her life when people had hurt her, but a flood of memories came rushing through. She heard Pamela come back inside. She waited for a knock on the door. It never came.

Five

Aimee sat at the café drinking coffee and editing her notes. Berlin kept eyeing her and refilling her coffee on a more than regular basis. Nic came in the back door to the kitchen and Berlin picked her up and put her on the counter.

"I have a plan. Want to help?" Berlin asked, looking her straight in the eye.

"Sure. Can I have a chocolate milkshake if I do?"

"Yes. In fact, I want you to take one to Aimee, and then I want you to make her laugh."

"Is she sad?" Nic asked, eyeing the table.

"I think so. But she's not talking about it. I'm depending on you to help her feel better," Berlin said, putting her hands on Nic's shoulders.

"I'm feeling a lot of pressure. I might need some French fries too."

"Deal. Now go out there and be your naturally charming self."

"Okay."

Nic set two chocolate shakes on the table. Aimee looked up and smiled.

"Hi, I took the liberty of ordering," Nic said.

"Did you put it on your account?"

"Of course. I'm a little behind because I've been busy at school."

"I could pick up the tab," Aimee offered.

"No, it's my treat," Nic said, seriously.

"If you insist."

Berlin brought over a heaping pile of French fries and a bottle of ketchup.

"I love French fries," Nic said, shoving three in her mouth.

"Me too."

"Are you feeling blue?"

"What?" Aimee asked.

"Do you have your period?"

"Nic!"

"That could make you blue," Nic said, matter-of-factly.

"You're five. How can you know about periods? Never mind. You know about sex, why not periods? Nic, what's left for you?"

"The psychometrics of objects . . ." Nic said, giggling.

"What!"

"Just teasing. Emerson taught me to say that whenever I find myself in a jam. Have some more French fries."

~ ~ ~ ~ ~

Berlin looked over at Nic and Aimee laughing. It's amazing what a child can do. Still, Berlin couldn't help wondering what was wrong with Aimee. She was certain it had something to do with Pamela, and she wished she could help.

"See you later, Berlin. I'm going to walk Nic home."

"Sure, honey."

Nic gave Berlin a hug and whispered, "Did I do okay?"

"Yes, darling."

"Want to come in?" Nic asked, when they reached her front porch.

"No, I should go home."

" 'Cause you're really busy?"

"Yeah, lots of work to do. Thanks for the snack," Aimee said.

"It was my pleasure."

Aimee walked back down Beckman Hill to the Main Street and across to the bookstore. The light was on and she decided she'd go buy a book. Crystal smiled at her when she walked in.

"Hello, stranger. Looking for some night reading material?"

"How did you know?"

"You're in a bookstore," Crystal ventured.

"Good answer."

Aimee went to find a book by Camus. She found *Resistance, Rebellion, and Death.* Whenever she was depressed she read either Camus or Mishima. Then she went to find one by Mishima. She'd started to read Mishima when she tried to find the culture she was born out of but not into. Memory had the cursed tendency to retrieve other painful moments into the present as if to remind her that life was a giant cesspool of unpleasantness, and happiness only a temporary, inflatable raft.

"Not exactly light reading material. Yikes!" Crystal said, as Aimee paid.

"Well suited to the mood, I assure you," Aimee replied, sticking the books in her backpack.

"I'm just about finished here. Want to go have a beer?"

Aimee wavered. "All right," she said, thinking she wasn't ready to go home yet.

They walked to the Canteen, and Crystal got them beers. Aimee sat back against the red Naugahyde booth and eased herself into the cool darkness of the bar.

Crystal lit a cigarette.

"Want one," she asked, offering the pack.

"Sure," Aimee said, taking one.

"I didn't know whether you smoked," Crystal said.

"A closet smoker, really. Pamela smokes and I sneak drags."

"They get you kind of high then."

"Yes, and for a stimulant they sure relax you," Aimee replied.

"Is this your first book by Camus or Mishima?"

"No, actually both of them will finish off a series."

"Why do you like them?" Crystal asked.

"Because they understand about misery."

"And you're in need of that right now?"

"Yes," Aimee replied, peeling the label off her beer.

"Are you okay?" Crystal asked.

"I'm trying to be."

"It happens more than we like to think. This fisticuffs business between women. Sometimes it happens only once, shocking both people back to their senses," Crystal said, lifting Aimee's T-shirt and looking at her arm.

"What about the other times?" Aimee asked, twisting her beer bottle around.

"The other times it keeps on and it gets worst, like the first time gives license for the violence to happen again and again."

"So do I get out now?" Aimee asked, thinking back to other moments of near violence and knowing she wasn't exactly a stranger to such fits of violent anger, either.

"Depends on what you think she's capable of."

"I don't know."

"Are you scared?" Crystal asked, firmly.

"A little," Aimee said.

"You should be."

"It put something between us that wasn't there before."

"Thumping on your partner does that. It's not something that should ever happen, but when it does you really need to think about causes. Violence isn't born of nothing. It's a festering."

"So healing or amputation . . ."

"Your choice."

"Right now I'd like another beer."

"Sure thing," Crystal said, flagging down the waitress.

Aimee ended up having four beers, a shot of tequila, and half a pack of cigarettes. Crystal told her the tale of her life with women, which was the reason for moving to New Mexico and living alone. She was still a lesbian. She just didn't practice it.

"Let me get this straight. You're a nonpracticing lesbian."

"Don't get me wrong. I love women, but I can't live with them."

"Perfectly understandable," Aimee replied, "considering what you've been through."

"Girlfriend, you have troubles, you come see me because most likely I've been through it," Crystal said.

"Don't be surprised if I take you up on it."

"I won't. Be safe tonight. You could crash at my place."

"No, I'll be okay."

"Just remember it's an option. Any time."

"Thanks, Crystal."

"You're a nice lady, Aimee. Don't forget that."

"I won't."

Pamela was up when she got home, and she saw Aimee look at her furtively as she slid through the front door.

"I wasn't with Lauren," Aimee said.

"I didn't say you were," Pamela replied calmly, even though she'd thought about it a hundred times.

"Listen, Aimee," Pamela said, getting up from the couch.

"I just want to go to bed. It's late."

"I know, but come here."

"No, I've got to pee and I want to get cleaned up," Aimee said, making her way to the bathroom.

Pamela sat back down. She listened as Aimee showered and then crept off to bed in the spare room. She wanted to go in and hold her and whisper a thousand *I'm sorry*s, but she knew the boundaries. Trying to make amends was not in the cards tonight. She curled up on the couch and tried to think, tried not to feel, tried not to want things she couldn't have. She hated being wrong, and she knew she'd been nothing but wrong.

~ ~ ~ ~ ~

Lauren called Emerson in the morning to remind her to pick up Aimee.

"Okay, no problem," Emerson replied.

"Thanks. So I'll see you two around ten then," Lauren said, putting her suit coat on and feeling the excitement of the challenge to manipulate the people with real money into helping her. And anticipating the added pleasure of seeing Aimee. The week had been too long already, and had Aimee been a single woman Lauren would have sent her flowers every day.

"Lauren?"

"Yes, Emerson?"

"You need to be careful. I don't want to see you hurt."

"I know. Thanks for being concerned, but I trust her. She's not taking me anywhere I don't want to go."

"Okay, just checking," Emerson replied stoically.

"I'm a big girl, Emerson. I can take of care of myself," Lauren replied.

"Gotcha," Emerson said.

Aimee sneaked past Pamela, who was sleeping on the couch. She quickly scribbled a note telling her that she was going to Santa Fe with Emerson and that she would be back later that evening. She waited on the porch for Emerson, who came rolling up shortly in the old red pickup, the back stuffed with crates. She handed Aimee a coffee when she got in. Aimee smiled.

"Thank you," Aimee said, taking a sip.

"It's early. I thought we both might need a jump-start."

"What's in the crates?"

"Some smaller sculptures to put in the all women's show Lauren is running at the gallery. I'm putting you to work when you get there," Emerson said.

"Can I take some photos? I brought my camera so I could

get some shots of Arial and the others at the commune for the book."

"Sure. Good publicity. I think Lauren is going to plug your book to the philanthropists as a selling point. I hope that's okay?"

"Wonderful," Aimee replied, nestling back into the seat and conjuring up visions of Lauren.

The philanthropists had already arrived by the time Emerson and Aimee rolled into town. Lauren was busy filling them in on the day's agenda. She looked across the room at Aimee as she and Emerson unloaded the crates. Aimee smiled, and Lauren's eyes sparkled with glee. She looked beautiful in her pale yellow silk suit, the quintessentially elegant and intelligent businesswoman. A woman who got what she wanted. Oh, that she would want me, Aimee mused. Had she spoken her thought, Emerson would have replied, but oh, my darling one, she does. But what is unsaid is what should be said and what is spoken a poor substitution, Aimee thought glumly.

"Boy, for such a skinny gal you sure got some arms on you," Emerson said, playfully squeezing Aimee's arms. Aimee screeched involuntarily. Emerson looked at her, surprised. She lifted up Aimee's shirt to see the now bluish purple bruises.

"What happened?"

"It's nothing, really," Aimee said.

"Did Pamela do that?"

Aimee looked away, trying to conceal guilt and implication.

"Are you all right?"

"Yes."

"Is that all she did?" Emerson inquired.

"Yes, she didn't mean to. Please don't tell Lauren," Aimee pleaded.

"I won't," said Emerson. "You're sure you're okay?"

"Yes, I promise."

"Okay," Emerson replied, confusion clouding her face.

Lauren introduced them to the committee of well-heeled philanthropists. They toured the gallery and then made plans to meet at the commune and take a look at the facilities. Arial would coordinate the tour and introduce the artists. Together Lauren and Arial hoped to get much needed grant money. Lauren could then increase gallery space, show more art, and thus create more revenue for everyone.

"Aimee, I know my stunning company will be sorely missed on the ride out, but why don't you go with Lauren and I'll get a head start and warn the rest, okay?"

Lauren smiled appreciatively at Emerson.

"So how has your week been?" Lauren asked, opening the car door for Aimee.

"Productive and very social. I had dinner with Nic at the diner and drinks with Crystal and did a lot of editing, which is my most unfavored part of the creative endeavor."

"I can only imagine," Lauren replied sympathetically.

"I'm going to try to take some photographs of the women at the commune today."

"That sounds wonderful."

"The book needs more visuals," Aimee replied.

"Did Emerson tell you about us plugging you into the money types?"

"Yes."

"Is that all right with you?" Lauren asked.

"Of course. I'm flattered."

"I like it when you're flattered," Lauren said, smiling as

she entered the interstate, checking in her rearview mirror to see if the entourage was following.

"Why?" Aimee said, flicking through Lauren's CD collection and picking one.

"Because you look very pretty in that state."

"Thank you," Aimee said, tracing the veins in Lauren's hand as it rested on the stick shift.

Lauren felt her touch acutely, like an electric shock that quivered in her veins and filled every part of her. She looked over at Aimee and then turned her hand palm up, opening her fingers. Aimee's cool, thin hand slid gently into her own. Lauren closed her eyes for a second and tried to suppress the shudder of absolute delight that enveloped her.

"Are you okay?"

"I'm wonderful . . . now."

"Good." Lauren clicked the CD in, and they both settled back to enjoy.

"You always pick the perfect song," Lauren said.

"You always have the right CD."

The tour and meet-and-greet went smoothly at the commune. Emerson managed to be cordial. Aimee and Arial orchestrated an incredible performance of information and impromptu photo shoot.

"You're a genius!" Lauren said.

"What do you mean?" Aimee asked, unloading her camera.

"Because the photo part flowed so well into the info part. Nobody got bored, and I think money bags was really impressed."

"I was just taking advantage of an opportunity," Aimee said, blushing.

"I have to pick up some stuff in town and I shan't bore Aimee with that, so when you take her to Lantana's for lunch, will you get me a grilled chicken sandwich to go?" Emerson instructed.

"Excuse me?" Lauren said.

"You're taking Aimee to lunch. Thin people need to eat. Right?"

"Right. Aimee, may I take you to lunch?"

"Please."

"I'll be back in a while. Take your time."

Lauren beamed at Emerson. She whispered to her on the way out, "You're a good friend."

"Remember that next time I piss you off."

Aimee began to wander the gallery. Lauren sat on the edge of her desk quietly watching her.

"Aimee, come here a minute, please," Lauren said.

"What?" Aimee said, coming closer.

Lauren lifted the sleeves of Aimee's T-shirt. Aimee felt her heart pounding, thinking back to other times when people would see the marks her mother had left. Depending on the response, it was a measure of love. It was the reason her father made her mother leave. Lauren looked at the bruises and winced.

"She hurt you. Why didn't you tell me?"

Aimee looked away, thinking, because I love you and I don't want you to think I'm a battered woman looking for an easy way out.

"Aimee . . ."

"I didn't want you to worry."

"How can I not worry? Look at these," Lauren said, holding Aimee's arms gently. Aimee looked down.

"I bruise easily," Aimee said, trying to smile.

"This isn't funny."

"I know."

"I can't believe you didn't tell me," Lauren said, color rising in her face, her voice pitched.

"I'm sorry," Aimee stammered, feeling suddenly helpless, victim and perpetrator rolled into one soggy mess. "I didn't know what to do . . ." She felt tears building up, and the pained look on Lauren's face made matters worse.

"Come here," Lauren said, holding out her arms.

Aimee fell into them gladly, memorizing each detail, Lauren's smooth white silk shirt, her breasts close to her own, her scent, body pressed against body, energy flowing between them, speaking their own secret language of promises yet to be filled.

"I didn't want you to think that you shouldn't see me. I couldn't bear that," Aimee murmured into Lauren's chest.

Lauren took Aimee's face in her hands, "That will never happen. I'll be there for whatever you need."

She pulled Aimee closer. Then she pulled away.

Aimee looked up at, surprised.

"I'm sorry, I'm being self-indulgent."

"Indulge me some more," Aimee said, pulling her close. Lauren closed her eyes and held her.

"Are you hungry?" Lauren asked.

"Very," Aimee said smiling. "Thanks for making me feel better."

"My pleasure."

Lantana's was packed, but Lauren's favorite waiter, Raul, found them a nice table anyway, one on the veranda overlooking downtown. He brought them a pitcher of margaritas, smiled graciously at Lauren, and told her to flag him when she was ready.

Aimee studied the menu.

"Any suggestions?"

"Their chili rellenos are to die for," Lauren replied.

"That sounds good," Aimee replied.

Lauren ordered the same thing, as well as Emerson's chicken sandwich.

Raul raised an eyebrow. "Are we hungry today?" he teased.

"It's for a friend," Lauren said, laughing.

Aimee sighed in relief. It seemed Lauren could be distracted from the ugly moment of earlier. Aimee searched for a topic to keep up the ruse.

"I got the publisher to give me an extension on the book so that I can include the art community in it. I'm really excited. I'm going to stay a little longer because I don't want to go back and find out I need more information."

"What about school?" Lauren asked.

"I'm off for the year. Sabbatical, remember?"

"I didn't know that. Are both of you staying?"

"No, Pamela has only sublet her apartment for the summer. Mine is indefinite. A friend has it, and she'll go as long as I want," Aimee said, refilling their margarita glasses.

"You and Pamela don't live together?" Lauren asked, confused.

"No, this is our first attempt, and you can see how well that's going," Aimee replied sardonically.

"How long have you been together?"

"Three years."

"And you've never lived together?" Lauren asked.

"I suppose in the world of attach-the-U-Haul-on-the-second-date lesbians we're an anomaly."

"It is rather unusual," Lauren said.

"We just never got there. I guess we both needed space, and then we went past that. You don't do that, do you?"

"No."

"You hate to date."

"I do. I want to wake up every morning next to the woman

142

I love and have dinner together every night, make a life together."

"What about the fear of the ordinary?" Aimee inquired.

"No fear. Only the fear of losing."

"Are you ready to be in love again?"

"With the right person."

"What a lucky woman she will be," Aimee said, feeling Lauren's hot stare.

"But does this elusive being want to be lucky?"

"I can't see how she would be anything but elated at having such an incredible woman love her," Aimee said, studying her fingers as they wrapped around the stem of her glass.

"And to be loved in return."

"Oh, she would love you. Where is she then?" Aimee said, looking around.

"Don't you wish sometimes that we could all say what we're really thinking and feeling and not be frightened at the outcome?"

"That would be approaching the shores of sane, grown-up, well-adjusted behavior."

"It would," Lauren said.

"I don't think as a species we're ready for that."

"Aimee?"

"Yes."

"I have only one request for the elusive being."

"What is it?"

"It goes back to an old thing. When Jill and I first fell in love, we slept together. When we had to tell our partners about falling in love, they mistook sex for love, thinking that we lusted after each other and that's what tore everything apart, and it wasn't. It would have been better if we had ended those other things first. It would have been easier on everyone."

Aimee nodded. "I think you're right, because that's what people focus on. They think you got bored and wanted something new and that hurts them more than if you could say look, I'm sorry, but I found the love of my life. I didn't mean to hurt you, but this is bigger than us. Love is irreconcilable when it's that strong."

"Precisely. Aimee, what do you really want?"

"I want love to be more than sex and tolerance."

"More than the sum of its components."

"Yes. Can it?"

"Yes," Lauren replied confidently.

"I need my faith renewed."

"It will be."

Aimee smiled.

Lauren stretched her hand across the table. Aimee took it gently.

When Emerson returned to the gallery, Lauren and Aimee were standing close to each other and examining the art work. Emerson spotted her grilled chicken sandwich and began munching on it, wondering how it would all end. She'd never seen Lauren look so happy.

Emerson thought back to the days when she had stolen Hope's heart away from Pamela. The mixture of guilt and elation had been confusing, but she knew no matter the consequences that to give Hope up would have done irreparable damage to her heart. There was no turning around on her internal highway, only fast driving and a myriad of sights and smells, touch and sensation, that no amount of reason, compassion, or conscience could forestall.

When you're hooked there's no undoing line, but the thought of Pamela being left alone again lingered, and Emerson inwardly cringed at the idea of yet another broken heart. How to judge? How to set the scales to find what is best, knowing that love gently sticks her toe on the scale in favor of what is true, not what is just.

"All right, ladies, it's time to go," Emerson said, doing a two-pointer with her trash into the garbage can.

"I'll be up end of the week," Lauren said.

"Good," Aimee said, tearing herself away.

"Well, aren't you going to give her a hug? I won't look," Emerson teased.

Lauren took Aimee in her arms. "Are you going to be all right?"

"Yes," Aimee said, nestling her face in the crook of Lauren's neck.

Emerson talked Aimee into staying for dinner. Nic was ecstatic. They sat in the backyard, drank beers, and told Hope of their day. Hope didn't inquire why Aimee wasn't with Pamela. She seemed to intuitively know that they spent more time apart than together. Her life with Pamela had been similar, and she felt grateful that she was no longer living like that. She wanted the fullness of a family, of a life spent with your partner, not fleeting glimpses, not just bed, but all of it. Later, Emerson told her how good Lauren and Aimee looked together.

"They're friends, but more than that," Emerson said.

"Like we were in the beginning," Hope replied.

"Exactly.

"What are we going to do?" Emerson asked.

"Let the astral goddess decide who gets what she deserves."

"What do you think she'll decide?" Emerson asked.

"That the hard-hearted go lonely," Hope replied.

"She's a harsh mistress."

"Emerson, you can't let love go untended. It goes bad if you do."

"I know," Emerson said.

Aimee managed another day of avoiding Pamela, wondering at the ease of living with someone you didn't see. She lay on the bed with arms outstretched, Mishima on one side, Camus on the other, a female Christ sacrificed to all the ugliness humankind was capable of. She thought about other times when books had been her only friend, the voice of sanity in a crazy world, when her parents had been fighting and she lay huddled in her room trying to read her way out of her life.

She had lied to Crystal. She'd read all their works, but these two books touched her the deepest. She needed to be touched if only to remind her there was more than surface.

Pamela knocked on the door.

"Aimee, I want to talk," Pamela said.

"Leave me alone."

"Come on. How long do you expect to go on like this?"

"As long as it takes."

Pamela tried the handle. The door was locked.

"Aimee, please unlock the door. I need to talk to you. This is ridiculous. You're acting like a child. I just want to talk. I won't do anything."

"I'm not ready to talk."

"Just let me see you, please," Pamela pleaded.

"No."

"Dammit!" Pamela said, hitting the door hard. She popped the lock, and the door opened.

Aimee coiled up in ball and grabbed a book, hurling it in Pamela's direction. It knocked her in the side of the head. She raised Mishima as a second defense.

"Why did you do that?" Pamela said, rubbing her head.

"You broke the door."

"It was an accident. I won't hurt you," she said, sensing Aimee's fear. "Now put the book down. I'll leave you alone."

Aimee put the book down as a sign of good faith.

"We'll talk later, okay?" Pamela said, backing out of the room.

"All right."

Lauren took the glass of wine Hope offered her. She had a refill before she had the nerve to say what was on her mind. Nic had gone off to play, so there was no longer an excuse for not discussing grown-up topics.

"What's wrong?" Emerson asked.

"Why should something be wrong?" Lauren asked.

"You have that distracted, perplexed look."

"It's a quandary. I can't decide if it's any of my concern, but I can't help thinking I need to make it so."

"What's bothering you, Lauren?" Hope asked patiently.

"It's Aimee."

"Yes."

"About the other day?" Emerson queried.

"Yes."

"Did she tell how it happened?"

"Yes, I feel like I'm half to blame for it. If she'd gone home on time, Pamela wouldn't have gotten angry," Lauren said.

"That's no excuse," Emerson said.

"What are you talking about?" Hope asked, refilling all their glasses.

"You didn't tell her?" Lauren asked.

"I didn't want her to worry," Emerson replied.

"Tell me," Hope said.

"Aimee has two perfectly bruised rings around her arms

147

where Pamela had her raised off the floor and pinned up against the wall," Emerson blurted.

"What!" Hope said, her face getting red.

Emerson winced and muttered, "This isn't going to be pretty."

"Did she ever hurt you?" Lauren asked.

"Only once. She slapped me. I made her swear she would never hurt anyone like that again."

"Do you think this is the first time something like this has happened with Aimee?" Lauren inquired, wondering if perhaps Aimee had told them something she was afraid to tell her.

"I don't rightly know. Aimee seemed pretty passive about it," Emerson replied.

Hope grabbed the car keys.

"Where are you going?" Emerson asked.

"To have a talk with Pamela."

"You're mad?" Emerson asked.

"Very. There are a lot of things I can put up with, and no relationship is perfect. But wife beating — or partner bashing or whatever you want to call it — is not acceptable, and I refuse to sit here and pretend it's not happening. Aimee is a small woman and she must have been frightened half to death. And she's staying in that house with that . . . monster."

"Honey, do you want me to go with you?" Emerson asked.

"No, I'll be fine."

They heard the car door slam.

"This is not good," Lauren said.

"No."

Pamela was surprised to see Hope. "Hey, stranger, what brings you to these parts?"

"Is Aimee here?"

"No."

"Is she coming back soon?"

"I don't know," Pamela said. She couldn't tell Hope that Aimee wasn't hanging around much these days.

"What did you do to her?"

"What do you mean?"

"You beat up on her," Hope said, feeling her face grow flush.

"I didn't mean to hurt her. It was kind of an accident."

"You just kind of slammed her up against a wall?"

"Did she tell you?"

"Why? Are you going to thump on her for telling your nasty little secret?"

"No," Pamela said, backing away.

"People see things, Pamela. They saw what you did."

"Is it bad?"

"You haven't seen her?"

Pamela leaned up against the couch and ran her hands down her thighs. She looked back up at Hope. "She won't let me near her."

"Good for her," Hope said, beginning to pace.

"Well, it doesn't exactly make it easy to fix things."

"Do you want to fix things?"

"Yes, I love her."

"You have a funny way of showing it."

"I didn't mean to do it. I swear. I've never done anything like this before. I just . . . I don't know what happened. We were fighting . . ." Pamela started to cry. "I just wanted her to stay still and talk to me," she sobbed.

"Now, don't do that," Hope said, starting to lose her nerve with the cascade of tears.

Pamela found a tissue and tried to compose herself. "How would you feel if you came home to see your sick girlfriend and she wasn't there and didn't come home for hours because she was with another woman? I was scared and angry. I didn't mean to hurt her, and I don't batter her. She'll testify to that. She hit me with a book, and it was an accident. This isn't what it appears. I know it looks bad, but it's not about abuse. I swear."

"For sure. Promise me you won't hurt her again."

"I won't. I didn't mean to hurt her the first time. Hope, everyone fights."

"All right. I can see how things might get out of hand sometimes, but this is not a good sign," Hope said.

"I don't want to lose her."

"I have an idea," Hope said.

"What?" Pamela replied, blowing her nose and looking perfectly miserable.

"Does Aimee have a favorite dinner, you know, the kind you die for, probably one you fixed when you wanted to show her how much you loved her?"

"Lobster bisque," Pamela answered.

"Boy, she doesn't come cheap, does she?"

Pamela shook her head.

"Come on. Let's go shopping."

"What for?"

"Stuff for dinner. The way to a woman's heart is still through her lower regions," Hope said. "It'll make you feel better."

"I don't think this is going to work."

"It's all we've got," Hope said, pushing Pamela out the door.

Aimee passed the flower shop. She'd been in a wretched funk most of the day. She was torn between feeling guilty for throwing the book at Pamela and scared about losing part of herself by resuming their relationship. This could be an easy way out, but she knew it wasn't right either. She stood with her face pressed against the glass. She could walk past and continue her life as a fugitive, or she could go inside and buy a dozen roses: to take them home, to take them with her to some unknown corner of the globe, to take them to Lauren's doorstep, or to lie down in them and bleed.

Would she run like she always had? From Pamela, from Lauren, from any and every connection that fortune promised her? Or would she stand and finish one love, and begin another, quivering at the thought of connection but willing to try. She knew that being with Lauren would take all of herself. Leaving part of herself with Pamela would not do. She opened the door, and the bells attached to it rang out. Was she entering heaven or hell?

The kitchen window was steamed over, and Pamela had stripped down to shorts and a tank top. Dinner was in full swing when Aimee walked through the front door carrying a dozen yellow roses. She felt duplicitous because she had also sent twelve white lilies to Lauren. The lady at the flower shop had winked and teased her about being a busy girl.

Pamela, looking timid and vulnerable, smiled at her. "You haven't eaten yet have you?"

"No, I haven't. These are for you," Aimee said, handing them to Pamela. "To say I'm sorry about hitting you with the book."

Pamela looked at them and burst into tears. "I'm so sorry. I don't deserve these."

"Shh," Aimee said, taking her in her arms. "It's okay. It's going to be okay," she said, stroking Pamela's hair and wiping the tears from her cheek. She kissed her forehead softly.

Pamela looked at her. "Will you forgive me?"

Aimee swallowed hard. The existential question. Lauren and their lunchtime promises made, about to be broken, flashed through her mind. Now didn't seem the time to bring all that up. She'd hurt Pamela, and Pamela had hurt her. Could she be in love with one woman and falling in love with another? Pamela kissed her neck, looked pleadingly into her

151

eyes, and Aimee succumbed. She knew the day was coming, but it wasn't today.

"Yes. Let's make dinner."

Pamela smiled so brightly it hurt Aimee to look at her.

"I got our favorite movie."

"That's nice. That's good."

And it was like old times and it was good, like when they first met. Time, T. S. Eliot's the end following the beginning came to mind as Pamela drew Aimee near and enticed her into the bedroom. Every amorous move made Aimee think of Lauren, made her feel guilt and longing rolled into one confusing conundrum. And as Pamela made her come, she thought of the end. End following the beginning.

Lauren sat straight up in bed, sweating. She'd been dreaming of Aimee, and something bad had happened. She couldn't remember what, but the sense of dread enveloped her. She lay back in bed, wishing she could call and say all the things that propriety kept from being spoken. Is she all right? Had Pamela hurt her again? What is she doing living in that place with that woman? What is she doing there? What am I doing here?

Six

When Aimee woke up, the sunlight was sneaking beneath the blind and dancing across the sheets. She rolled over and felt the empty space next to her. She opened her eyes.

"Fuck," she said softly, thinking just once, just this once, couldn't Pamela be here. Aimee rolled over, wondering at the immensity of double beds when you found yourself alone in them. She got up and turned the coffeemaker on. Her wine headache of last night sat firmly lodged in her temporal lobe. No note, no I love you, no I went to fetch breakfast I'll be right back, only the empty sloughing sound of her own two feet.

She got coffee and turned on the computer, wishing she had other companions. Wishing for another life, a better one,

one full of soft, fuzzy, warm things she didn't have names for yet. But she could feel them dancing around in places she didn't know how to get to yet, but she knew she wanted to. She was ready now, but was a better life ready for her?

Aimee logged on to the Internet and e-mailed Hannah. She knew Hannah had her laptop with her and would welcome a message from a long lost friend. If anyone could help her decipher her duplicitous behavior, Hannah could. She sat down and composed the entire story of her summer. It made her feel better telling someone. Reading the words on the screen as she typed them made everything more real, made her look at what she was doing. Perhaps advice from Hannah would help her make the right decision.

Lauren paced back and forth with the phone. Her dream last night clung to her and all she could think of was Aimee. She had dialed Aimee's number fourteen times, and each time it had been busy. She called the operator. The line was in use.

"Dammit!" Lauren said, jamming the phone into the receiver.

"Who are you trying to call?" Emerson inquired.

"Aimee, but the line's been busy all morning. How long can you talk on the phone?"

"Depends on who you're talking to. She's probably got admirers all over town by now."

"She does not!"

"Little defensive this morning? You two really need to do something about how you feel for each other before this whole mess turns into an ugly obsession."

"It's not ugly."

"What is it then?" Emerson asked.

"Confusing."

"You forgot *obsession*."

"All right. It's a confusing obsession," Lauren admitted.

"What are you going to do about it?"

"It's not like I can walk in there and say listen, I really want you so you need to dump Pamela and come live with me."

"Why not?" Emerson said, raiding Lauren's fridge, her initial purpose in coming over. She'd reached the point of starvation. She pulled out a moldy pack of bread.

"You should really throw this away," Emerson said, putting it back in the fridge.

Lauren snatched it away from her and threw it in the trash.

"How come you never have any food in here?" She pulled out a jar of pickles. Lauren always had pickles. It was their one epicurean similarity.

"Because I don't live here."

"Yeah, I'm sure the Santa Fe fridge is stocked."

"I'm having an emotional crisis and all you can talk about is food," Lauren said, fishing a pickle out.

"Do you think our pickle fetish has anything to do with penis envy?"

"No! Now help me out here. What am I going to do?"

"About your pickle fetish?"

"No, about Aimee!"

"Well, if you really want to talk to her, I'd just go over there. But in the long run I think you're going to have to get rid of Pamela. Now, you have two choices: poison or divorce. If you choose poison I'd read a lot of Agatha Christie novels first."

"I can't just drop in," Lauren said, ignoring Emerson's other helpful hints.

"Sure you can. It's a small town. We do that here," Emerson said, pushing her toward the door. Lauren looked at her, uncertain.

It's amazing how love can render the most staunch weak in the knees, Emerson thought, chuckling to herself. She could laugh now. She'd been there. The past is often amusing in the eye of the present.

Aimee answered the door wearing a sport bra and boxers, a baseball hat turned backward, and a mouthful of ice-cream cone. The mournful cries of U-2 blared out as Aimee let Lauren in and then went to turn down the stereo.

"Hi," Aimee said, looking obviously pleased.

"You should be shot."

"Why?" Aimee asked, quickly tallying her current list of misdemeanors. Fucking Pamela's brains out last night definitely sat high. What could she say, I only thought of you while I was coming into the wild blue yonder? She still hadn't figured out why she had slept with Pamela. One more for old time's sake. Sick and twisted, but probably true.

"For having a body like that and eating ice cream on a regular basis," Lauren said, pinching Aimee's stomach.

"Want a bite?" Aimee said, putting some on her finger and pointing it in Lauren's direction. "It's cherry jubilee."

Lauren took it and sucked Aimee's finger.

Color rose in Aimee's face, "Oh my."

"Got a woody?" Lauren asked, her eyes smiling.

"Not yet, maybe you should try again."

Lauren had another fingerful.

"Oh yes, that's it."

Lauren gently bit her finger.

"What's that for?"

"For being a tease."

"I can't help myself. You bring it out in me," Aimee said, taking Lauren's hand and guiding her into the living room. "How have you been? I've missed you."

"I've been trying to call you, but the line has been busy. I got scared," Lauren blurted.

"I was online e-mailing an old friend."

"You're all right then?"

"I'm fine. A better question might be, what's up with you?" Aimee asked, sensing Lauren's anxiety.

"I had a bad dream last night," Lauren confessed.

"About me?"

"Well, yes, like maybe she was hurting you again."

"Actually, I threw a book at Pamela the other night," Aimee said rather matter-of-factly.

"Did you hit her?"

"Yes . . . felt kind of bad afterward, seemed the thing to do at the time. But we're speaking to one another again. I suppose that's good," Aimee said, thinking, I can't tell her good-bye if we're not talking.

Lauren looked at Aimee and then the dozen yellow roses on the dining room table.

"Are you always this ambivalent?"

"No."

"Good."

"Why, do you think I'm a bad lover?"

"Indifferent perhaps," Lauren said.

"It depends on whom I'm in love with," Aimee said, reading the confusion in Lauren's eyes.

"Are you in love with Pamela?"

"Anymore or once?"

"Either, I suppose."

"I thought I was once. I think now I've realized that I have only been in love twice in my life. I know I loved Honour."

"Who is the other woman?"

"Someone I shouldn't have."

"Why?"

"Because I live with one woman and pine for another. How can you trust someone like that?"

Lauren stood looking at her, as if trying to read what was written in her eyes. Aimee was about to cross the room, take

Lauren in her arms, and whisper, I love you, I love you, I love you.

Just then the screen door opened. Pamela walked in, surprised to find them there. Even though they were standing across the room from each other, Aimee and Lauren looked guilty.

Lauren recovered quickly. "There's a carnival in town tonight, and everyone is going. Did you two want to go?"

"I have a conference call coming in around six and then . . . I don't know."

"You don't have to go, if you don't want to," Aimee said.

"I don't want to or you don't want me to?" Pamela said.

"Why don't you two think about it and, if so, everyone is meeting at the café at seven," Lauren said.

"I'll walk you out," Aimee said.

"This is a mess, and I'm sorry," Aimee said.

"I don't mean to put you in a bad way . . ." Lauren said, leaning up against the car.

"Maybe I can run away from home and join the carnival," Aimee said, trying to smile.

"Do you want to live with her?"

"No, but I need to learn to say good-bye, and I'm scared," Aimee said.

Lauren took Aimee in her arms.

"Please don't cry. It's okay. I'll do whatever you want," Lauren said, looking into Aimee's eyes.

"You touch me in ways I've never been touched before, and I wish my life wasn't such a wreck. It's just that I've got to finish some things."

"I know. And I understand."

"I'll see you tonight then?"

"Yes. Don't get in trouble though."

Aimee nodded.

"Thanks for the flowers," Lauren whispered in her ear, lingering a moment.

Aimee turned red and swallowed hard. "You are so beautiful."

Lauren got in the car and smiled. "So are you."

Aimee waved as she drove off.

Pamela was seething.

"What, are you two dating?"

Aimee laughed. "Wouldn't that be nice. No, we're not dating but we are friends and, no, I haven't slept with her, nor will I do so while I'm still with you."

"Are you still with me?" Pamela asked.

"Do you want me to be?"

"Yes," Pamela said.

"Is that why you got up and left this morning, making me feel like another one of your completed projects? In case you haven't noticed, I'm a human being, not a question to be answered, a problem solved. I'm supposed to be the woman you love and the only thing we do well together is fuck. And when that's done you're out of here."

"Aimee . . ." Pamela said, coming toward her.

"No, leave me alone," Aimee said, grabbing her backpack and leaving.

Aimee stood on the sidewalk for a few seconds and then went back inside to change. She couldn't go downtown in her underwear, no matter how attractive Lauren thought she looked dressed that way.

Pamela had shut down the computer and was using the phone. Aimee shook her head in disgust. Is it possible to hate love? she wondered. She decided to go see Hope.

Aimee felt foolish going into the bookstore. Why she was going to see her lover's ex-lover to talk about things seemed ludicrous, but Hope was the only one who would understand.

Hope and Emerson stood at the back of the store. Hope was trying to pull a book away from Emerson.

"You're not reading this. You don't need to read this. It's not about us, and you've got to stop it," Hope said.

"I can't help it. Every time I look at Aimee I see those pictures of people hurting each other," Emerson said.

"Emerson, sometimes you have to look life in the face and not in a book. People hurt one another sometimes. Pamela hurt Aimee and Aimee hurt Pamela and they both feel bad about it. We have to let it go. They will sort it out. Now give me the book," Hope said.

Emerson handed it over.

"I don't know if I'm ready to look life in the face. Things just make more sense when they're in print and someone, somewhere, far away wrote them," Emerson said.

"You can do this," Hope said, pulling her close.

The front door clanged open, and Hope and Emerson looked up.

"I've got to go," Emerson said. She snatched the book from Hope and ran for the front door.

"That's shoplifting," Hope called out after her.

"Put it on my account," Emerson said, racing by Aimee.

"Hi and bye. Everything okay?" Aimee asked, thrusting her hands in her pockets.

"Minor dispute over literary tastes," Hope replied.

"I see."

"What's up?" Hope asked.

"Can we talk?"

"Sure. Come have some iced tea."

It was Crystal's day off, so Aimee pulled a stool up to the counter and sipped her tea. Hope sat on the stool behind the counter.

"So what's on your mind?" Hope asked.

"I know you know about the shit that's been coming down between Pamela and me, and I guess I'm just confused

160

because I still have feelings for her but I'm in love or I think I'm in love —"

"With Lauren," Hope said.

"Yes. I didn't mean for this to happen, and I feel guilty. But then I keep thinking that if a relationship is strong, other people can't come between it. Right?"

"Well, yes and no."

Aimee rolled her eyes. "I hate love. It's stupid and confusing and makes dupes of us all, and it's probably all hormones anyway."

"It's not, Aimee. Yes, sometimes people come between other people and sometimes it's just a stronger kind of love. It doesn't mean you have to negate the original love. What's making this so hard for you?"

"How can I leave her? I feel like I'm waiting for her to fuck up so I have a reason. That's not fair to her, and I'm sure she feels it. It's like the other day. I saw Lauren and all I wanted to do was put my arms around her and tell her how I feel, and then I spend the night making love to Pamela and getting them both confused. What am I doing?"

Hope smiled sympathetically. "Falling in and out of love simultaneously."

"That's sick," Aimee said, looking hopelessly around her. "Timing is everything, isn't it?"

"It would be nice to be single when the woman of your dreams comes walking in, but then —"

"But then lesbians usually aren't single."

"We believe in the pathology of two."

"What am I going to do?"

"When you're ready you'll leave."

"What about Pamela?"

"She's a big girl."

"I feel so bad," Aimee said, running her hands across her face.

Hope stood up and took Aimee's hands in her own, "I know that you loved Pamela."

"I thought I did."

"And it is not like you didn't try to give her your heart. But you can't make someone something they're not."

"I keep thinking that if I give her one more chance maybe things will change."

"Aimee . . ."

"I know. I wait until she pushes me to the very brink, and then I'll go. Right?"

"Yes."

"What do I do in the meantime?"

"Live as best you can and keep your bags packed."

"Is that what you did?" Aimee asked.

"Yes, and I felt as hopeless and evil as you do right now."

"I don't want to hurt her, but I keep thinking that to stay with her is to lose a good chance at happiness."

"It is."

"So I'm not really doing her a favor by staying if my heart is elsewhere," Aimee said.

"No, you're not." Hope said.

The door clanged open and two women came in.

"I should go," Aimee said, hopping down from the stool. "Thanks for being such a good listener."

"Any time. Remember, you have family and friends here."

Aimee nodded, then rushed out to the street.

These women, this town . . . Aimee had never felt she belonged anywhere, until now.

She stood outside the studio, knowing that Lauren was most likely upstairs, and she wanted to go see her. But somehow that felt like running from the arms of one lover into the arms of another. Standing there looking up at the old building, she knew she didn't want to do that. Standing there watching puffy white clouds come over the top of the building, she felt calm, like what was supposed to happen would. Things fall apart and then they get put back together. She would go home and straighten up her life.

When Aimee got home she kissed Pamela on the cheek and then went to work on her outline and text. Aimee looked up once or twice and found Pamela staring at her.

"Aimee . . ." Pamela said.

"What?" Aimee said. She finished the sentence she was writing and looked over, giving Pamela her full attention.

"I'm sorry about leaving this morning. I just felt good and didn't want to wake you. I didn't mean to make you think that we made love and everything was fine. I know there are things we have to work on. I love you," Pamela said.

Aimee felt her stomach knot up into a tight ball. It always happened like this. One person falling out of a relationship and the other realizing too late that she wanted to save the sinking ship while the drowning lover wanted only to escape from pain and longing. It made her question wanting to be in love again. She thought of Crystal, the nonpracticing lesbian.

Lauren was a wonderful woman, but could Aimee stand to one day look across the room at Lauren and feel the same sickening sense of loss she was experiencing with Pamela? She shuddered involuntarily. Was it any wonder love was so difficult when a vain goddess and her capricious son were its ambassadors?

"Are you cold? I turned up the a.c.," Pamela said, going to check the temperature.

"No, I'm fine."

Pamela wrapped her arms around Aimee, who was staring blankly at the computer monitor. Pamela nuzzled her face in Aimee's neck.

"Last night was wonderful, and I'm sorry I let you down."

"It's okay, really," Aimee said, kissing her cheek and trying to smile. "We're fine. Let's just forget about it."

163

Pamela nodded, but Aimee could see doubt lingering in her sad eyes. Aimee didn't know how to assuage it, so she let it go, knowing this was the first step in saying good-bye. They went back to work, and the strange tempo of their lives resumed.

Pamela didn't go to the carnival, and Aimee tried not to feel guilty for going. But as Pamela put it, going out with the girls was a social thing that Aimee needed and Pamela did not. And for the time being Pamela no longer questioned Aimee on her friendship with Lauren. If you say you're not sleeping with her, I believe you, Pamela told her.

Aimee felt easy with Lauren, and they happily pursued the perfect platonic romance. Aimee suspected Lauren wasn't any more ready than she was to jump into another relationship. They were doing an almost unheard of thing in the realm of lesbian love: getting to know each other first before they fell passionately into bed.

Emerson was pacing back and forth in Lauren's office. They'd been talking about business when Emerson promptly switched gears.

"I don't get it."

Lauren was well versed in abrupt changes in conversation with Emerson. "Get what?"

"What you two are doing."

Lauren looked legitimately confused. "What are you talking about?"

"You and Aimee. So you two get to hang out together, and as long as you don't sleep together, everything is kosher with Pamela."

"Basically," Lauren said, taking a sip of coffee and trying

to keep complete calm across her face. Her feelings for Aimee were too new and ultimately too precious to be discussed, and she only got them out when she was alone, when she could touch them gently and try to assure them that everything was going to work out fine. They were tentative little creatures, and she had to be careful.

"You're just friends then?"

"Yes."

"I thought you loved her?"

"I do."

"Then what are you waiting for?"

"For her to be ready. For me to ready."

"Meanwhile . . ."

"We hang out, we have fun, and we get to know each other. I don't want to have an affair with her. I want to *live* with her. I want to *be* with her," Lauren said, feeling her face get hot.

Emerson looked at her. "All right, I can understand that."

"Why are you so concerned?"

Emerson poured more coffee and took a sip.

"Well . . .?"

"Because it makes me think of what happened between Hope and me."

"With Pamela?"

"Yes."

"Was it messy?"

"I felt bad."

"I feel bad," Lauren admitted, thinking this was the second time she had stolen someone else's lover.

"It's not easy falling in love with someone else's wife," Emerson replied.

"No, it's not."

"I'll be there for you."

"Thanks," Lauren said, holding out her arms.

"I thought I was your one and only," Hope said, coming in.

"You are," Emerson said, looking over Lauren's shoulder.

"Then what's this about?" Hope teased.

"Aimee," Emerson said.

"Oh yes, our adorable Aimee," Hope said. "We had a talk the other day."

"You did?" Lauren asked.

"We did," Hope said.

"What did she say?"

"Buy me lunch?" Hope said, looking coyly at Lauren.

"Anything," Lauren said.

"All right," Hope said.

"What did she say?" Lauren prodded.

"The whole thing or the gist?"

"Everything," Lauren said.

"Well, she feels bad about Pamela but . . ." Hope said, "Lunch with a lot of wine?"

"Hope," Lauren said, knowing her face was gaining color by the minute and her heart was beating quickly.

"But she's madly in love with you and her bags are packed," Hope said smiling.

Lauren picked her up and swooped her around.

"Are you serious?"

"Of course. Do you think I'd mess around about something like that? In fact, I'm meeting her for lunch. Want to come?"

"You beast," Lauren said, putting her down.

"Does that mean yes?" Hope teased.

"You're tormenting me," Lauren said.

"I am. Ready?"

"More than ready."

Hope took Lauren's arm on the way down the stairs, "I know this is hard and it would be wonderful if Pamela wasn't in the picture, but I know you'll make Aimee very happy, and that's what counts. Pamela will survive. Believe me, she's had enough practice."

Lauren looked at her, uncertain. That was another one of the difficulties of her new situation. Aimee leaving a partner reminded her of all the havoc of when Jill and she had to rearrange everyone's life so they could be together. Falling in love again was forcing her to deal with some long buried hurts. She wasn't as ready as she thought to be in love. She wanted to do this right, but she didn't know for certain what *right* entailed.

Pamela watched as Aimee shoved things in her backpack. She was trying to be patient, trying to ride out the rest of the summer, but it wasn't easy. She felt like everyone was on Aimee's side. Most of the people they had interviewed for the book felt more comfortable talking to Aimee, so Pamela had been relegated to taking notes. And then Lauren was always around. Playing second fiddle was difficult for her.

To top off the summer, Pamela was not pleased that the triplets were slated to arrive any day. She was going to inevitably look like the bad guy when the party girls came to town and her relationship with Aimee was tentative at best. It was all becoming more than Pamela could handle. She felt like she was living in a building on the verge of implosion.

She knew that she needed to say that she couldn't keep living like this, always wondering when Aimee was going to leave, knowing there was nothing she could do to stop it.

And Aimee needed to respond that she knew and it was unfair to both of them to keep up the charade but that she felt bad for wanting out, for letting her down. Instead, they were fighting about going to a concert.

"I told you about this weeks ago. Lauren is coming to get us."

"But I've got all this stuff being faxed in, and I want to be here to get it," Pamela said.

"You promised we'd go."

"This is important."

"So's this."

"It's a fucking concert!" Pamela said.

"It's more than that. It's a celebration of women's music. It's support for the community, for the same women you're writing about."

"I don't understand why you're getting so upset."

"I wanted you to be there."

"I'm busy," Pamela said, knowing she was lying. She didn't want to go because it was painful to see Aimee and Lauren together.

"You're always busy."

"At least someone is."

"Don't go there. I'm doing my part."

"What you've decided your part is," Pamela said.

"Damn you," Aimee said, walking out the front door.

"Aimee wait! Do you always have to leave?" Pamela said, standing out on the porch.

Aimee stopped.

"I don't want to go because I feel uncomfortable around Lauren," Pamela blurted.

"Why didn't you just say that in the first place? Why say all those other things? Why can't you tell me how you feel? I can't do this anymore."

"Aimee, please don't go. Let's talk."

Aimee looked at her with tears in her eyes. "I'm sorry I let you down. I thought I could do it, but I can't . . . I just can't."

Pamela stood there, not knowing what to say.

~ ~ ~ ~ ~

Lauren was trying to get up Morgan Street when she saw Aimee. She looked at her watch. It was still early. What was Aimee doing? She looked in her rearview mirror at the sea of cars behind. She couldn't possibly flip a U-turn.

"Shit!"

A delivery truck pulled out in front of her, leaving the yellow loading zone temporarily vacant. She pulled in. Getting across the street proved another difficult task. Lauren waved, smiled, and cajoled her way between cars. After a brief trot, she caught up with Aimee. She touched her hand.

"I told you we don't have anything more to talk about," Aimee said, before she turned around. When she saw Lauren, she apologized. "I thought you were Pamela."

"I'm glad I'm not."

Aimee looked at her and burst into tears. Shocked, Lauren took her in her arms.

"Maybe I should just pack up and go back to New York. I can't take this anymore," Aimee said.

Lauren pulled her tighter. "Don't go. Please don't go."

Aimee looked at her, confused. Lauren wiped away her tears.

"I love you, Aimee," Lauren said.

Aimee nestled into Lauren's neck.

Three women who looked identical sat in a Volkswagen Westfalia watching the whole thing.

Honour looked over at Hannah. "I'd say Pamela's out of the picture."

Hannah nodded.

"She sure traded up, that's for certain," Holly said, jabbing Honour.

"So I see," Honour said, wondering to herself how she ever let Aimee get away from her.

They watched Lauren take Aimee's hand and lead her through the throng of vehicles to her car. They pulled into traffic.

"I guess we'll see them at the concert," Hannah said, studying Honour's face.

~ ~ ~ ~ ~

"Are you okay?" Lauren asked as they got out of the car.

"Yes, thank you," Aimee said, taking Lauren's hand. "I don't mean to be so needy right now."

"Oh, Aimee, it's not like that," Lauren said, touching her cheek.

Aimee rested her face in Lauren's hand. Lauren felt the overwhelming desire to kiss her. She felt stirring down deeper. Lauren smiled, thinking this meant she could do it. She could feel desire for another woman other than Jill. She could think about making love to Aimee. She could have another life after all.

"You make me happy, and you make me feel things I didn't think I was capable of," Lauren said.

Someone swept Aimee up from behind, holding her like a bride cradled in the arms of her beloved. Honour planted a deep kiss on Aimee, bringing color to her face. Lauren suppressed the tinge of jealousy she felt rising. As she looked at the two other mirror versions of Honour, it dawned on her who they were.

"My darlings, you're here. I thought you might have just been toying with me," Aimee teased, as she gave Hannah and Holly a hug.

"This is Lauren."

They shook her hand.

"Well, for shit's sake, let's get a beer and start the party," Honour said, giving Lauren a tap on the back. "You're awfully pretty," she said to Lauren.

"We must toast Aimee's good taste in women, shan't we, sisters," Honour said, taking Aimee's hand and dragging her toward the nearest beer stand and purchasing two extra large beers for all.

"How have the races been going?" Aimee asked.

"Beauty, Honour is tops in her class, and Nike is renewing her contract," Hannah replied.

Honour beamed.

170

"The sisters are not far behind," Honour said, wrapping her arms around them.

Lauren stared at them. She found it disconcerting to look at three people who looked exactly alike.

They found a seat on the lawn as the music got started. It was fun to watch people do double takes of the triplets, and Honour did her best to charm Lauren, who inevitably found herself quite charmed. When Honour went for another beer run between sets, she insisted Lauren go with her.

"So you'll take good care of my little darling, yes?" Honour asked as they waited in line.

"Who?"

"Aimee! You two look good together. Just got to get rid of the wife, eh?"

Lauren blushed.

"Hate that woman. Caused nothing but havoc in Aimee's life. You'll be good for her. I can tell already," Honour said, handing Lauren a tray of beers, a tray of nachos, and five salted soft pretzels and an order of curly fries. Lauren was trying balance everything as Honour managed the other two trays of beers.

"You don't believe in making two trips," Lauren said, tucking the bag of pretzels under her arm.

"This is just for now. We'll need more beer. Where is that snatch of a wife of hers anyway?" Honour said, taking a quick look around.

"Pamela didn't want to come."

"That figures. She's such a cunt. You like to have fun, and fun we shall have," Honour said, smiling broadly. "You're a lucky woman, you know. Aimee is simply wonderful. I still rue the moment I shot that arrow. I would have loved to have spent the rest of my days with her. It's hard knowing you let the one you should have loved forever slip away. Remember that."

Lauren nodded, thinking this was the most energetic, forthright, bizarre woman she had ever met.

"Sweet Jesus, we'll be fat as pigs tomorrow," Holly said, as Honour handed her the provisions.

"Day off and we're carbo loading. I want to have fun," Honour whined.

"Still out of control as ever," Hannah whispered to Aimee.

"Group rules, no secrets," Honour lectured Hannah. "Besides, don't make me feel like I have to chaperon you two."

Hannah and Aimee both blushed, while Lauren felt a pang of remorse for knowing a little too much. She'd contemplated Aimee's past and knew that it must have been wild. It made her wonder. She and Jill had led such tame lives. But she remembered the old advice of sowing wild oats and making better partners. When she looked at Aimee, she didn't give a damn about what went on before. She was here now, and she loved her, and that was all that mattered.

"I wonder where Hope and Emerson are?" Aimee said, taking Lauren's hand.

"I doubt we'll ever find them in this crowd," Lauren said, trying to scan the amphitheater.

"Sorry I messed things up."

"I'm sure they figured out something happened. We'll catch up with them later," Lauren reassured her.

They drank a lot more beer. Aimee was enlisted on one of the beer runs, much to Lauren's dismay. Hannah tried to soothe her fears.

"Honour knows when she has lost. She will always love Aimee, but Honour is not in Aimee's best interest for a stable, sane life. I place my bet with you," Hannah said, squeezing Lauren's hand.

Lauren breathed easier, sipped her beer, and questioned Hannah and Holly about their summer exploits.

"So Lauren is really hot," Honour said, as they waited in the long beer line.

"Yes," Aimee said.

"And you like her, right?" Honour asked.

"I love her."

"Big trouble in paradise."

"Pamela was never paradise," Aimee said ruefully.

"What are you going to do about it?"

"Go home and pack," Aimee said.

"Wow, this serious."

"Really serious."

"What if I told you I was still madly in love with you?"

"I would say you were too late," Aimee said, putting her arm around Honour's shoulder.

"I thought so."

"I miss you though," Aimee said.

"I miss you too. But I don't begrudge your happiness."

"Thanks, bud."

The last song of the concert was a slow song. The lead singer instructed everyone to grab a partner and give the universe one big dash of love. Honour shoved Aimee into Lauren's arms and grabbed the nearest available lesbian, who was more than thrilled. The dance began, and Aimee's and Lauren's bodies melded into one until Honour shoved both of them off to one side.

"Wife alert!" Honour said, grabbing Holly and Hannah to serve as a shield.

Aimee looked over her shoulder to see Pamela, Hope, and Emerson, followed by Katherine and Berlin moving in their direction. Aimee wasn't certain they hadn't seen them. She didn't care. She wanted to get out of there as quickly as possible with no altercations.

They piled in the van and then sat looking at one another.

"Where are we off to?" Honour asked.

"Good question," Aimee said.

"How about the liquor store and then the loft? They won't think of there for a while, and then Emerson will fend them off," Lauren suggested.

"We should probably get a hotel room since it doesn't look like staying at your place is a good idea," Hannah said.

"Yeah," Aimee said, thinking of a variety of scenarios at home, none of them pleasant.

"I need to get the car," Lauren said.

"Okay, where is it?" Honour said, starting the van.

The triplets followed Lauren and Aimee to the store and then to the loft, where the party began anew. They drank beer, ordered pizza, listened to music, and explored the wonders of being fugitives.

"I like this," Holly said, looking out the loft windows at the huge harvest moon rising up over the mountains.

"It's Lauren's home away from home," Aimee said.

"Where's home?" Holly asked.

"Santa Fe," Lauren said.

"Let's go there tomorrow," Honour said. "I love Santa Fe."

"We could," Lauren said, looking at Aimee.

"How long do you guys have?" Aimee asked.

"The weekend," Holly said. "We need to be in Salt Lake City by Tuesday for the Guts Man Race."

"Let's go then," Lauren said.

"I don't have any clothes," Aimee said, feeling like a real fugitive.

"You can wear some of mine. They'll be a little big, but I have lots of belts," Lauren said, starting to feel the long night of drinking.

Aimee looked uncertain.

"There's no turning back, baby. It's time," Honour said.

"Okay," Aimee said, looking at Lauren for reassurance. Lauren took her hand.

"It'll be all right. I won't let anything happen to you," Lauren said.

"I need to go to bed," Hannah said.

"Yes, I think we've done enough damage for one night," Lauren said, taking up the role of hostess.

She found blankets and unfolded one of the couches and then they made up the other couch. That took care of three beds.

"I can sleep on the floor," Aimee offered.

"I don't think so," Honour said. "I know there's a double bed. We won't tell."

Aimee looked at Lauren. Lauren smiled. "I promise to behave myself."

"Shucks," Aimee said, bravely.

Everyone settled in. Lauren got Aimee a nightshirt and they cleaned up, and then they stood awkwardly at the edge of the bed.

Timidly, they both got in.

"It's not like we haven't slept together before," Lauren said.

"I know," Aimee said.

Lauren brushed her hair back. "I meant what I said. I love you . . . to the point of obsession, to the point of doing whatever it takes to be with you."

Aimee took her in her arms, nestling her neck. "I love you."

Lauren pulled back, looking deep into her eyes, as if trying to read what was written there. Aimee took her face in her hands and softly kissed her, their bodies drawing close.

"I have wanted to do that for so long," Aimee said.

Lauren pulled her closer, whispering, "I love you, I love you, I love you." Tears started to well.

Aimee brushed them from Lauren's eyes. "You are so wonderful. I feel lucky . . . and happy and sad and drunk."

"And tired. And I wish we didn't have a houseful of people."

"Me too," Aimee said.

"But we've waited this long . . ." Lauren said, kissing her again.

~ ~ ~ ~ ~

After Aimee fell asleep in her arms, Lauren stared at her face for a long time, thinking about past and future things, trying to talk to Jill, trying to tell her this was all right. And sometime in the middle of night, Lauren knew it would be.

Seven

They drove to Santa Fe, and Aimee tried hard not to think of Pamela. They stopped to get gas and Aimee called Hope.

"Hi," Aimee said.

"Good morning," Hope said. "What's up?"

"I need you to do me a favor," Aimee said.

"Sure," Hope said.

"I didn't go home last night, and the triplets are in town."

"Okay," Hope replied cautiously.

"We're on our way to Santa Fe for the weekend."

"To stay at Lauren's?" Hope inquired.

"Yes."

"Are you leaving her?"

"I think so," Aimee said, feeling the hard knot in her stomach grow tighter.

"Well . . ."

"I don't know what to do," Aimee replied honestly.

"I could tell her that you're staying in Santa Fe with the girls and that you'll talk to her on Monday."

"Do you think that will work?"

"It's the best we've got at the moment. She knows what's going on. You saw us last night, didn't you?"

"Yes."

"I'll take care of it."

"I feel so bad," Aimee said, starting to cry.

"It's over, Aimee. We all knew this was coming, right?"

Aimee sobbed.

"Aimee?"

"Yes?"

"You'll make yourself and Lauren very happy. Pamela will never be happy," Hope counseled.

"I know," Aimee said, trying to collect herself.

"It'll all work out," Hope counseled.

"Thank you, Hope," Aimee said, hanging up the phone.

Lauren came out of the gas station and saw Aimee. "Are you okay?"

Aimee nodded.

"You don't look okay."

Aimee fell into her arms and started to cry.

The triplets came up behind them.

"Remorse is an ugly thing," Honour said. She pulled a beer from the six-pack she was holding and handed it to Aimee. "So buck up and let's go. Time and distance will cure anything."

Aimee tried to smile and got in the car.

Lauren gave them the grand tour of Santa Fe. They had a barbecue on the patio, and the triplets and Aimee spent the rest of the afternoon soaking in the pool.

When Honour saw the pool she looked over at Aimee.

Aimee smiled. "A hundred bucks says you still can't beat me."

"You're on," Honour said, immediately disrobing.

They were both in the pool doing fast laps.

"Aimee was on the swim team in college. She always wins. Honour can't accept that," Hannah told Lauren.

They watched as the women swam laps until Honour gave up and surrendered.

"I see you still swim," Honour noted.

"Yes, as a matter of fact, I do," Aimee said, helping her out of the pool.

"So your incredible stomach muscles are obviously not a fluke of nature," Lauren said, handing Aimee a towel.

Aimee blushed. "Did I neglect to mention my swimming career?"

"You did," Lauren said.

"You have no idea of the things she's done," Hannah said.

"No, I don't," Lauren admitted.

"She's an amazing woman, and she thinks she's a piece of shit," Hannah replied.

"Why is that?" Lauren asked.

"Wait until you meet Mom and Dad, then you'll understand," Hannah replied.

"Is that true?" Lauren said, looking at Aimee.

"Psychologically speaking, yes," Aimee said.

They spent the rest of the day eating, drinking, and getting silly. Lauren liked having her house full of women again and having Aimee close with no time constraints, no worrying about getting her home so Pamela wouldn't be angry. It almost felt like Aimee lived there, and Lauren wanted that. Wanted to be with her, wanted to wake up every single morning with Aimee in her arms.

In the evening Lauren got everyone settled. She had a big

house with lots of room. They got the triplets to bed. Lauren looked at Aimee.

"There's still another bed, if you want it," Lauren said.

"I have a better question. Do you want me to stay in it?" Aimee replied.

Lauren took her hands, "No, I want you to stay with me. If that's all right."

Aimee studied her for a moment. "I want to be with you."

They talked deep into the night and held each other. Lauren could feel herself wanting Aimee as she touched her hands and face and listened to her, but she didn't want to push her into being lovers. She wanted Aimee to be ready.

She whispered to her, "I would really like to make love, but not now, not until things are settled and you're ready. Is that okay?"

"Yes, and thanks for being patient," Aimee said.

Aimee looked into Lauren's eyes, "Where have you been all my life?"

"Waiting for you," Lauren said.

Lauren watched as the van pulled out of the driveway. The triplets were dropping Aimee off in Heroy on the way to Salt Lake. Lauren was worried, but Aimee had told her she needed to take care of some things and would meet her at the loft for a late lunch. It'll be better if she shows up with us, Honour had assured her. Aimee had held Lauren tight and whispered that everything would be all right.

But now that Aimee was gone, an avalanche of conflicting emotions ran through Lauren's head. She wanted Aimee to stay with her; she was afraid of what Pamela was capable of; Aimee said she loved her, but it was hard to be in love and then have her lover gone the following morning.

The little, black voice in her head kept telling her she was just another one of Aimee's many lovers, one of which included her wife. Lauren told herself it was all right to be madly in love and horridly insecure. It was part of it.

Pamela stared at the computer screen. She didn't know what to think. On the one hand, Aimee had spent the weekend, albeit impromptu, with the triplets, in which case everything was fine. Hope, when she called, had said nothing to the contrary. On the other hand, Aimee had spent the weekend with Lauren, and they were now lovers. Pamela knew there would be no winning Aimee back then because she wouldn't have slept with Lauren if she thought they were still together.

When the van pulled up outside and she saw the triplets, her heart leapt. Aimee hugged them good-bye and kissed Honour before she came inside. Pamela tried to look calm.

"Did you have fun?" she asked.

"Yes," Aimee said. "It was good to see them again. I didn't think you'd want them here, so I thought it best to take them sightseeing."

"Thank you. That was very considerate of you. Look, Aimee, I'm sorry about the other day."

"It's okay. Over and done with," Aimee said, resting on the corner of the couch.

"I can't believe we almost got this whole book thing organized," Pamela said.

"Yes, that's a good thing," Aimee said, straightening her desk and packing up her computer. She could feel tears forming.

"What are you doing?" Pamela asked.

"Packing," Aimee said, looking at her. "I'm sorry. I'm so sorry, but I can't do this anymore."

"You're leaving?" Pamela said, incredulous. "You're just walking out?"

"I don't know what else to do," Aimee said, going to the bedroom.

Pamela followed her.

"That's it. We're over," Pamela said, watching Aimee shove clothes in her duffel bag.

"I'm sorry," Aimee said, not looking up.

"Are we going to talk about it?"

"I don't have anything left to say."

"But I love you. Doesn't that count for anything?"

"It's unfortunate. It would be easier if you hated me," Aimee said, zipping up the duffel and wiping her tears with the back of her hand. She headed for the door.

"You're in love with her, aren't you?"

Aimee stopped at the front door. She turned. "I loved you, Dr. Severson, and I don't regret it. And there were times when I thought we could make it. I didn't mean to hurt you, but I can't stay. I'm sorry."

Pamela stood crying in the middle of the living room, listening to the sound of footsteps on the porch and then the glide of Aimee's bike as she took off down the street.

Aimee rode across town, thinking that in the course of twenty minutes she had made one woman incredibly sad and another very happy. She climbed the stairs to the loft.

"What are you doing?" Lauren asked.

"Coming to take you to lunch," Aimee said, setting down the heavy duffel bag.

"That's an awfully big purse," Lauren said, looking at the bag.

"I'm leaving."

"You're leaving. Where are you going?" Lauren said, distress written across her face.

"I don't know yet, but would you like to come along?" Aimee said, contemplating for the first time that she'd walked out of her house with no other plan than getting away from Pamela.

"Yes, anywhere," Lauren said, swooping her up in her arms. "I love you."

Lauren pulled away, "Did you talk to Pamela?"

"In a manner of speaking."

"What do you mean?"

"I went home and told her I was leaving her, which was rather redundant considering that I was packing."

"You went home and packed and it's over just like that?"

"I didn't know what else to do. I only know I love you."

Lauren pulled her tight.

"Can you still love a woman that leaves her lover that way?"

"Promise me you won't leave me like that," Lauren said.

"I won't need to."

"You know that already?"

Aimee nodded. "I found the right one."

Lauren smiled and picked up her bag.

"Where are we going?"

"Home," Lauren said.

"Are you sure you want to do this?"

"I'm positive."

Hope sat on the couch and poured Pamela another scotch.

"Are you okay?" Hope asked.

"No," Pamela said, clinking the ice in her glass.

"I'm sorry. I wish there was something I could do."

"Don't say that."

"What?"

"I'm sorry. Aimee kept saying that. I'm sorry, I'm sorry, while she packed. How could she just decide like that? That today she would come home, take her things, and go off. Just walk out the door with a duffel bag, and that's it."

Hope looked down guiltily at her glass, remembering she had done the same thing, just walked out of Pamela's life. She thought about the philosopher Hegel saying that history repeats itself, the first time as tragedy and the second time as farce. She felt like a farce sitting there, trying to console the inconsolable when she knew all along that Aimee was leaving, that she was learning to leave, and that Pamela couldn't see it. Couldn't see far enough ahead to avert the disaster, and now she was like the deer stunned immobile by the headlights of a truck labeled *heartache*. What good was she doing, sitting there ruminating over a dead philosopher's words and drinking scotch?

"Why don't you come have dinner with us? Get your mind off of it."

"*It*, as in Aimee. *It*, as in love gone awry. *It*, as in wondering if she's fucking Lauren at this very moment. I love her. How can she do this?"

Hope refrained from saying, *Because she had to. Because to stay was emotional suicide.*

"Come for dinner."

"No, I think I need some time alone. I'll be fine. You go. I know they're waiting for you," Pamela said.

"Are you sure?"

Pamela nodded.

Lauren drove them to Santa Fe. The sky was incredibly blue, and Aimee felt an overwhelming sense of relief, like Scotty had just beamed her up from a very nasty planet and now she was safe, warm, and happy. She looked over at Lauren and squeezed her hand.

"Where do you want to go for lunch?" Lauren asked, knowing the fridge at home was completely empty.

"That sweet, little Mexican restaurant you took me to before."

184

"Feel like reminiscing?"

"Yes, only this time after lunch I get to go home with you."
Lauren smiled.

When they got back from lunch, Lauren tried to suppress the urge to pick Aimee up and carry her into the bedroom. Instead, they were holding each other in the kitchen. Lauren looked over her shoulder and saw Aimee's big, black duffel bag on the couch. Her mind kept singing over and over, she lives here now, she lives here now.

"I love you," Lauren whispered in Aimee's ear.

Aimee pulled away and looked at her, "Then show me."

Lauren lead her upstairs.

"All I ever wanted was you."

Aimee kissed her.

Lauren slowly took off Aimee's shirt, watching her. Aimee quivered as Lauren kissed her breasts. Lauren undressed her and pushed her gently toward the bed.

"You are so beautiful," Lauren said, kissing her neck. "I've wanted to touch you from the moment I met you."

"But it's not polite to grope a stranger," Aimee teased, pulling Lauren's clothes off.

"No, it's not," Lauren said, easing down on Aimee and feeling their bodies touch. She closed her eyes for a moment to savor the feeling, to always remember what it was like to feel the length of her lover's body as she covered it with her own. She didn't want to forget a single instance. She felt like she was being given a second chance to learn to love, without hurry or frustration, without ego and drive and all those weird childish things she'd put Jill through. This time she wanted to make it right, to take all the things Jill had tried to teach her and put them to use.

She felt Aimee pull her in tight, trying to reach for her, to taste her, touch her, feel her. They stared into each other's

185

eyes and kissed, letting tongues collide and wrap around each other for what seemed like forever. Lauren could feel the wetness between them growing, but she kept watching Aimee. She made her way down Aimee's body, sucking her nipples until they grew hard, flicking little kisses across her stomach, while Aimee ran her hands through Lauren's hair. Lauren took Aimee in her mouth, feeling the heat and wetness, licking slow and long, hearing Aimee's breath grow rapid, hearing the soft, low moans of pleasure. She waited for the right moment, when she knew Aimee was almost there, and she glided her fingers inside, coming up closer to Aimee, wrapping Aimee's legs around her, feeling Aimee pull her to her, her body growing tight and then the cry, the long, sweet fire of love. Lauren watched as Aimee's hand grabbed the sheet and twisted, and Lauren knew Aimee had reached that final sweet agony.

They lay together, sweat making them glisten. Aimee smiled.

"Come here," Aimee commanded.

Lauren lay on Aimee's chest and listened to Aimee's heart pound.

Aimee brushed Lauren's hair back and stroked her face gently. She ran her hand down Lauren's smooth stomach. She felt Lauren quiver.

"I should warn you. I'm going to come the minute you touch me," Lauren said apologetically.

"I have an idea," Aimee said, pulling her closer. "We'll name the states alphabetically."

"What?"

"Starting with the letter A, as in Alaska. It will keep you focused, and then touch me here, and that will serve as another diversion," Aimee said, taking Lauren's hand and placing it between her legs.

"Did you learn this in the self-help section at B. Dalton's?"

"No, on *Dharma and Greg.*"

"You amaze me," Lauren said.

"Alabama . . ." Aimee prompted.

"Arkansas," Lauren responded, trying to focus.

"California," Aimee said.

"Delaware," Lauren said, feeling Aimee go deep inside her. They got to the letter *K* before they both came.

"See, wasn't that fun?" Aimee teased.

"Best geography lesson I've ever had," Lauren said as she lay quivering in Aimee's arms.

"I doubt your retention will be any good tomorrow. Pop quiz and all that," Aimee said.

"I'll remember everything, I assure you," Lauren said.

Aimee ran her fingertip around Lauren's nipple. She eased Lauren on her back.

"There are things I've been remembering, places I'd like to explore . . ." Aimee said, gently kissing her stomach. "Would that be all right?"

"I think my heart rate is back to normal. I don't know for how much longer though," Lauren said as Aimee's tongue traced the inside of her thigh.

"Hmm . . ." Aimee said, pulling Lauren's hips toward her mouth. With grace and precision, Aimee sucked and licked, and then glided her fingers inside Lauren.

Aimee explored Lauren's body, getting to know the places she had yet only imagined. She was gentle with Lauren. Lauren made her feel gentle, made her feel like she was making love and not fucking. It wasn't the raw kind of power of taking someone else's body and making it your own. No. With Lauren, Aimee felt the tenderness of wanting to share the experience, not to master her lover. She wanted to make Lauren feel incredible, not make her pay for loving her, not make her want for things she couldn't have.

She wanted to give Lauren everything. If Lauren had

asked Aimee to rip out her heart and hand it over, Aimee would have done so gladly.

Then she could feel Lauren inside her, and she was inside Lauren, uncertain anymore who was who, rather two becoming one, feeling Lauren pull her tight, feeling herself crying out and then doing it again, like they were both experiencing passion for the first time and it made them insatiable. She heard Lauren whispering again and again, "I love you, I love you."

Later, Aimee lay in Lauren's arms, watching her sleep, watching her chest rise and fall, her skin smooth against Aimee's face, her look peaceful, her look that of being well loved and of sleeping in your lover's arms. Thoughts of the strange day came floating in. Of leaving Pamela, of driving to Santa Fe, of spending the afternoon making love, of ordering take out and eating it in bed, and of making love again. Talking about everything, including about learning to let go and about needing time and space. It seemed Lauren understood everything, how to give the things Aimee longed for. It was so perfect it frightened her.

Suddenly she felt like the incompetent one, like she would be the one to fuck up this love affair, and then she understood how Pamela must have felt. How she never knew what to do to make things right and how hard that must have been, like walking in a minefield, anticipating the blow, envisioning everything coming apart but still forced to trudge through, wondering and waiting.

Aimee untangled herself from Lauren and went downstairs, trying to make her way quietly in a house still foreign to her. She experienced the fear of being given something perfect and not being worthy enough or able enough to sustain it. She felt her chest constrict, felt herself go inert, felt the tears come, felt all the dread of everything not well done in her life, not knowing how to love well enough, for creating the bubble of detachment she had enveloped herself in. Maybe the failure hadn't been Pamela's fault but her own? Maybe she brought it out in people. Maybe she was the one that drove them away.

Lauren rolled over and felt Aimee gone. She sat up, groggy from sleep. She looked around and instantly panicked. She got up hurriedly; the first thought in her head was that Aimee was gone. She found Aimee on the couch crying. Only then did her heart start to beat again. She put her arms around Aimee, feeling the sobs that racked her body.

"Shh . . . what's wrong?" Lauren said, pulling her tight.

Aimee gulped and tried to catch her breath. She looked at Lauren through tear-stained eyes. She tried to summon up the courage to tell her, to start the process of revealing her feelings, of slowly climbing out of her bubble to breathe outside air, good air, not the narcotic air of her secret world where bad things remained static, too anesthetized to hurt her.

"I'm frightened," Aimee said.

"Of what?"

"That this is too good and that I'll fuck it up. I won't be what you need. That one day you'll wake up and wonder why you're with me," Aimee said, feeling the words tumble out of her, gushing out of the bubble in one long stream of truth.

Lauren wiped away her tears. "Don't be frightened. I love you. I'll tell you what I need. All we have to do is talk, tell each other things, and we can do this. Oh my god, you are so incredible," Lauren said, holding her tighter, "Please don't doubt yourself. Just love me. That's all I want."

Aimee looked at her. "I do love you."

"I know you've got some things to sort out . . ."

"Baggage?"

"Yes, and I want you to feel free to talk about it, even stuff about Pamela. You don't have to hide things. I don't want you to hide them. That's how things go bad. We'll talk about things, and we'll tell each other how we really feel, not what we think the other wants to hear."

Aimee nodded.

"Come to bed," Lauren said, taking her hand.

Lauren held her, stroking her hair, until Aimee fell asleep.

Emerson sat at the counter of the diner and scowled at her plate.

"What's wrong? I made it just like you like it. Although why you insist on having your breakfast smile back at you is beyond me," Berlin asked, staring at Emerson's breakfast.

Emerson looked at her pancakes with the two eggs for eyes and a piece of bacon for a smile and felt bad.

"You're right. Having my breakfast smile at me this morning does seem perverse," Emerson said, turning the piece of bacon into a frown.

"What's wrong?" Berlin asked, leaning on the counter and looking straight into Emerson's eyes.

"I feel bad," Emerson said, swirling the yokes of her eggs around.

"Why?" Berlin prodded patiently.

"Aimee left Pamela yesterday."

"Why do you feel bad?"

"Because I started the whole thing," Emerson replied, looking the picture of guilt.

"All you did was introduce them. It's not like you threw them in bed together."

"Not that. Taking Hope away from Pamela. If I hadn't done that, then Pamela wouldn't be with Aimee and Aimee wouldn't have left her."

190

"Emerson you're being absurd and taking a much too grand stand on the whole thing. That's like blaming yourself for all the wrongs in the universe. Hope left Pamela for the same reason Aimee left her. They both found their soul mates. You can't deny that. Unfortunately, sometimes there's carnage," Berlin said, refilling her coffee cup.

"I still feel bad. Maybe I should take her a bagel and coffee. You know, just to see how things are going. Do you think that would be all right?"

"I think that would be nice. A gal needs friends in times like these. Did Aimee go to Santa Fe?"

"Yes."

"That's good," Berlin said, handing her a coffee to go and a bagel.

"Why?"

"Running into ex-lovers stinks for the first few months."

"I wouldn't know, mine just disappear into thin air," Emerson replied.

"Maybe that's better," Berlin said.

"Easier on the eyes, harder on the heart. You keep waiting for them to show up."

"And then one day you start to forget you ever knew them."

Emerson smiled. "Yes, I think that's the best part."

Hope looked up from the register to see Emerson flying in the door.

"She's gone!"

"Who's gone?"

"Pamela."

"How do you know she's gone?" Hope asked.

"I went by to see how she was doing. No one was home, but the front door was unlocked. I knocked and it kind of opened. I peeped inside, and everything was gone. She must have packed up in the night and headed out."

"I hope she's all right," Hope said, concern etched across her face.

"Do you think she'll call you?"

"I hope so."

"She probably went home, huh?" Emerson said.

"I'm sure. There wasn't much reason to stay . . . anymore."

"No," Emerson said, trying hard to block out the memory of coming home and finding Angel gone, but she could feel it rattling around in the back of her mind like a tin can tossed about by the wind.

"This isn't like when Angel left. Emerson, don't go there. This is not the same thing," Hope said, looking deep into Emerson's eyes and taking her hand. "This is different, someone else's life, two lovers that said good-bye. Okay?"

"Okay," Emerson said, starting to breathe normally again.

The sky was bright blue, and sunlight danced across the wood floor of the bedroom. Lauren smelled coffee and heard Aimee in the kitchen. She lay in bed and relished the moment, thinking of how often she'd dreamed of this moment and now it was real. She tried to bask in her joyful feeling, but she wanted to see Aimee. Lauren grabbed her robe and went downstairs, feeling like a child at Christmas who couldn't wait a second longer to start the day.

Aimee looked up from the stove and smiled at her.

"You're supposed to still be asleep so I can bring you breakfast in bed," Aimee admonished.

"I'm sorry, but I missed you," Lauren said, wrapping her arms around Aimee.

"If I'm going to live here, I do have one request," Aimee said, looking seriously at Lauren.

"Anything," Lauren said, trying not to have an instant anxiety attack.

"We have to have food. You have one egg in the fridge, that's it. Two women cannot survive on one egg. How have you been living all this time?"

"I don't like to eat alone," Lauren said, running her tongue around Aimee's ear. "We'll go grocery shopping, I promise."

"I'm going to hold you to that," Aimee said, as Lauren's hand slipped inside her robe and traced the outline of her breast. Aimee flipped the egg.

Lauren kissed her stomach and then took her in her mouth. Before Aimee knew it, Lauren had her on the kitchen floor and the egg was burning.

"Where are you going?" Lauren said, alarmed.

"Turn off the stove. I think we burned breakfast," Aimee said, reaching for the knob on the stove.

"I'll take you out for breakfast," Lauren said, pulling Aimee back to her.

When Aimee rolled off her, they looked at each other and smiled.

"I thought you said you didn't know how to fuck. That was fucking," Aimee said.

Lauren laughed. "I can't help it. You bring it out in me. Come on, let's go have a shower and get something to eat," Lauren said, helping her up.

"And then we go grocery shopping."

"Yes."

"Do you even know where the grocery store is located?" Aimee asked suspiciously.

"Of course," Lauren said indignantly.

"Do you know how to cook?" Aimee asked.

"Sort of. Do you?" Lauren replied, snapping Aimee with a towel.

"Maybe," Aimee replied.

"If I remember correctly, you needed help with the potato salad," Lauren recalled.

"I have a confession."

"Yes?" Lauren said.

"I know how to make potato salad. I just wanted to talk to you," Aimee said, trying not to blush.

"So you do know how to cook," Lauren said.

"Took culinary classes, toyed with the idea of becoming a chef," Aimee replied.

"Well, no wonder you are obsessed with food."

"No, I'm obsessed with making you breakfast, lunch, and dinner every day," Aimee teased.

"You'll make me fat."

"We'll work it off at night," Aimee said, pulling Lauren to her.

"I like that idea."

Lauren floated in a cloud of domestic bliss as Aimee put food and more food on an already heaping shopping cart. When they finally got to the checkout, the payment discussion ensued, with both of them attempting to pay.

"No," Aimee said, firmly.

The clerk was getting annoyed.

"But . . . I want to," Lauren said, pulling her debit card through the scanner.

"Look, it's an armadillo," Aimee said, pointing toward the produce section before Lauren could key in her PIN.

Lauren looked. Aimee slipped the clerk the money.

"That was shifty," Lauren said.

"I know," Aimee said, wheeling the cart out. "I am living in your house. The least I can do is buy the groceries because somehow I don't think you'll let me pay rent."

"You're right. But I don't feel comfortable doing the my-your-money thing either. So how about a joint checking account?" Lauren asked, hoping she wasn't going too fast, but she wanted to get the details out of the way and now seemed like the perfect moment. Otherwise, she would have to wonder about the arrangement, and that made her nervous.

"What if I'm a spendthrift?" Aimee said, loading the groceries in the trunk.

"I happen to know you own a bike, a laptop computer, and a duffel bag full of clothes. You seem like a minimalist."

"You're right."

"Do you have any more stuff in New York?"

"No," Aimee said. "I brought all my worldly belongings with me."

"I don't think I have anything to worry about. What do you do with all your money, if you don't mind me asking?" Lauren said, as it dawned on her that a professor with a good salary and no possessions must do something with her money.

"I'm a compulsive gambler," Aimee said.

Lauren's face dropped.

"You wouldn't love me if I was," Aimee teased.

"You're not, are you?" Lauren said, her face full of anxiety.

"Investment portfolio," Aimee said. "I never lived with anyone that I felt stable with. I didn't need many things. I didn't have any place to put them."

"You truly are a nomad," Lauren said.

"Not anymore," Aimee said. "I don't mean to torment you. It's just that setting up housekeeping is kind of weird."

"I don't want to pressure you," Lauren said.

"You're not," Aimee said, getting in the car. "People are just going to think we're extremely organized. In the course of two days, I've gotten divorced, moved in with my beautiful lover and we've ironed out the living details. So it's settled. We're married," Aimee said, making a ring out of the sales receipt. She took Lauren's hand.

"With this ring I thee wed," Aimee said.

Lauren kissed her.

"See, easy," Aimee said.

"Very easy."

"We're typical U-Haul lesbians. I've never been one of those," Aimee mused.

"Welcome to the island of Lesbos," Lauren said, pulling out of the parking lot.

"Are we going to start to look alike?" Aimee said.

"By the end of the week, probably."

Eight

Hope didn't call Lauren and Aimee, like Emerson wanted. She tried to explain to the overly anxious Emerson that Aimee knew Pamela could take care of herself and that if she was truly interested she would have called. Emerson wasn't convinced.

"Emerson, let's let the two lovebirds have a little time to just be in love minus the hassles," Hope said.

"I just think she should know," Emerson said, getting out the Pepto-Bismol.

"That's the third bottle this week. You're going to the doctor," Hope said.

"It's this thing. It gives me a stomachache."

"Why do you have a stomachache when this has nothing to do with you?" Hope asked.

"It's lesbian cosmic transference. It reminds me of . . . Angel," Emerson said, looking away.

Hope came to hold her. "You can't seek resolution through other people. You have to find it on your own."

"I'm hoping that if I experience enough resolution vicariously then it will rub off on me and I'll be cured. Will you call?"

"All right."

Aimee and Lauren walked in the door just as the phone stopped ringing. They had gone clothes shopping and out to lunch. The gallery was having an opening for Emerson's latest work. The duffel-bag queen, as Lauren had taken to calling Aimee, needed an outfit. They bought her a beautiful black suit.

"You look like Dana Scully with dark hair," Lauren said.

"Is she not the sexiest woman?" Aimee said, twirling in the mirror.

"No, you are," Lauren said, straightening the collar of the white silk shirt after Aimee had thrust the jacket on.

"I'm counting on you to help me maintain a polished exterior. You are looking at a woman who does not iron."

"You do clean up well. We'll send everything out to the cleaners," Lauren assured her.

They plopped the bags down. After purchasing the suit, Lauren had talked Aimee into getting a few more items.

"It's a good thing I'm staying or else I would be truly violating my one-duffel-bag rule," Aimee said, looking at all the bags on the couch.

"Having your own walk-in closet has already severely marred your nomad status," Lauren teased.

"That doesn't really count if it only has a few things hanging in it."

"No longer."

"The only way I'd be a nomad now was if I took you with me," Aimee said, looking overwhelmed and slumping down on the couch between the multicolored shopping bags.

Lauren laughed. "It's not that bad. Cut off the tags, wash the stuff, and you'll never know you acquired so much in one afternoon." She got a pair of scissors and hit the answering machine on the way to the couch.

It was Hope.

"Hello, you two. We miss you and wonder when you're going to come up this way again. Nic is ravenous for your attentions. Give us a call when you have time. Emerson is her usual thoroughly excited person about the opening of the show. She does promise to behave herself. We'll see. By the way, Pamela left town the same day Aimee did, and we haven't really heard from her, but I'm sure she'll call one of these days. Just thought we should let you know. So take care and we'll see you soon."

Lauren stood holding the scissors. She watched Aimee, who made a beeline for the back door.

"Aimee . . ."

"I'm fine. I just need a moment alone," Aimee said.

Lauren took three deep breaths. She heard the splash and went to look out the arcadia door. Aimee was swimming laps. That was okay. Lauren was slowly learning that Aimee swam when she needed to think. She picked up the phone and called Hope.

"Hello?"

"Hi, we just got your message," Lauren said.

"How is she doing?" Hope asked.

"She went swimming."

"Is that a good thing or a bad thing?"

"I think it's a good thing," Lauren replied, watching Aimee doing lap after lap. "She's an excellent swimmer."

"How are you doing?" Hope asked, sensing Lauren was distracted.

"I was wonderful until five minutes ago."

"I'm sorry. I figured she should probably know," Hope said.

"She should. Did Pamela take it rough?" Lauren asked. She'd been mulling that question over and over and beating herself up with the possible answers. Maybe things would be better if she knew.

"I went over that night. She wasn't in good shape, but that was to be expected. Emerson went to see her the next morning, and she was gone."

"She just disappeared?" Lauren said, feeling her heart beat quicken.

"That's Pamela's style. She wouldn't want anyone to see her lick her wounds. Don't worry."

"Are you sure?"

"You're as bad as Emerson in the guilt department. It should count for a lot that both you and Emerson took two nice women, who happened to be living with someone who wasn't making them happy or well-adjusted, and gave them the chance to be happy and loved. It's a good thing," Hope said, giving Emerson another look.

"You're right."

"But you still feel guilty?"

"I do. But when I hold Aimee in my arms, all I think about is how much I love her."

"Go do that then," Hope advised.

"She's still in the pool."

"Maybe you should get her out."

"Good idea."

Aimee looked up and saw Lauren holding a towel.
"Time?"

"Time," Lauren said.

"I'm not a bad person," Aimee said. Letting go of someone who was hurting her was not a bad thing. It was like her mother, it was like Honour, it was like all the memories that caused her pain. She tried to imagine those thoughts and feelings streaming behind her, leaving a trail of muddy water. If she swam far enough and long enough, she could leave the water clean, leave those people and those thoughts to form the delta of a past she had shorn. She could leave a place she never had to see again. That was all she wanted, a chance to start over, a chance to be carefree. She wanted the opportunity to love without pain, without anguish.

"No, you're not a bad person," Lauren said, offering her a hand.

"And neither are you," Aimee said.

"I'm not," Lauren said, striving for conviction.

"One day we won't remember her anymore."

"Can we start now?" Lauren asked.

"Yes," Aimee said, pulling her close.

"I got you all wet," Aimee said, looking down at Lauren.

"And you don't have any clothes on," Lauren replied, trying to suppress the urge to swoop Aimee up and carry her off to bed.

"Let's go take a bath," Aimee said.

"Together?"

"Together," Aimee said, taking her hand.

Lauren was always apprehensive when Emerson decided to attend one of the openings, but so far the surly artist was placated. Lauren kept filling Emerson's glass as well as Aimee's full of champagne. She had only meant to keep Emerson sedated, but Aimee was in the vicinity and it would have been rude not to top her glass off as well. It wasn't until Hope pointed out the raucous laughter of Emerson and Aimee as they stood near the long, back wall of the gallery did Lauren see her error.

"I think they're trashed," Hope said.

"I think you're right. The show is almost over, so if we can keep them from doing anything too obnoxious we'll be fine."

"I have an idea," Hope said.

"What?"

"Let's go flirt."

"With who?" Lauren said, instantly mortified.

"With them, silly," Hope said.

"I don't think I know how to flirt," Lauren said.

"I beg to differ on that account. Pray tell, how was it that you captured such a charming woman's heart?" Hope teased.

"Well, maybe I know how to flirt a little," Lauren said.

Later as she chased Aimee up the stairs to the bedroom, picking discarded items of clothing as they fell, Lauren was certain she knew how she'd captured such a charming woman's heart.

Aimee drew her to the bed, unbuttoning her blouse and kissing her stomach. She looked up at Lauren.

"Have I told you how much I love you today?"

"Not nearly enough," Lauren said, easing her body down on Aimee's.

The kitchen smelled like food when Lauren walked in. Having the chef cook on a daily basis was making Lauren go to the gym on a regular basis. She was seriously considering getting a treadmill installed for the gallery. Aimee laughed at her fears of fatness, but then she was the woman who went swimming every day for lengthy periods of time. The pool had never been so much used, and Lauren was beginning to wonder if she'd bought a house with a huge pool because somewhere deep in her psyche she knew Aimee was coming.

"It smells outstanding in here, and you look wet," Lauren said, noticing that Aimee was still wearing her bathing attire.

"How can you tell?" Aimee said, doing a perfect three-quarter French turn.

"My fears of fatness give me extra powers of perception. What are you making?"

"Something incredibly fattening, but I intend to engage in extracurricular activities later, so we'll work it off."

"I like that," Lauren said, putting her arm around Aimee's waist and smiling at her lasciviously.

The phone rang. Lauren pinched Aimee's butt and went to answer it.

Lauren came back with the phone.

"It's for you," Lauren said, with a puzzled look on her face.

"Can you put it on the speakerphone?" Aimee said, her hands in the dough for the calzones. "I'm kind of incapacitated at the moment," Aimee replied not giving a thought to whom it might be. She assumed it was one of the triplets.

"Okay," Lauren said, switching it over.

"I would appreciate it if you would notify me of your whereabouts. I do not appreciate having to track you down like a common criminal. You know I do not like that woman, and, getting no accurate information from her, I am forced to use other methods. I am not happy."

Lauren sat down, her body racing with complete total apprehension of what was next.

"Hello, Father, it's nice to hear from you again," Aimee said.

"Your mother is returning and wants to see you. I told her you were in Santa Fe. She likes the climate. She wants to have our family outing there. I was thinking lunch."

203

"Did you tell her she can drop dead?" Aimee replied, punching the dough forcibly.

"No. I did not. We will be there Tuesday. Please find an appropriate restaurant."

"I'm not going. I will see you but not her. Please relay the information," Aimee replied.

"This is unacceptable. Call me tomorrow with the time and place. Good-bye."

"I'm not going," Aimee said.

Lauren clicked off the phone.

"Meet the family," Aimee said facetiously.

"I want to meet your parents," Lauren said. "You've met my family."

"Your family is normal and well-adjusted. Mine is not, and you're not meeting them because neither am I," Aimee said, forming the calzones and stuffing them. She did not look up, and Lauren watched her acutely.

It wouldn't be the first time a lover inquired about her relationship with her parents, but this would be the first time it mattered. Even Honour was not that interested, but in college it was easier to be rebellious and disconnected from the kind of society that parents represented. Pamela had considered Aimee's father a rude, short man with an overly masculine nature to make up for being a small man, and so she crossed him off as not worth her time. He was part of the people she fought against in her battle with the patriarchy. But Lauren was different. She would want to know why.

"Why not? It's lunch. We can handle lunch," Lauren said lightly.

"No, we cannot handle lunch. Lunch is asking more than I can give. My father is making me an accomplice in his annual parade of guilt, and I'm not playing," Aimee replied harshly.

"Aimee, what's the big deal?"

"It's not a big deal because I choose to ignore it," Aimee replied, feeling herself getting flushed.

"They're your parents. You can't ignore them like that," Lauren replied.

"I can and I will," Aimee said, slamming the calzones in the oven. She turned to look at Lauren. This was not a topic for discussion.

"I don't understand," Lauren said.

"Nor are you ever going to. So I suggest you drop it," Aimee said.

"I thought we were going to talk about things," Lauren said.

"This is one thing I don't talk about, especially with you. You don't get it, do you? I never go. My mother meets my father once a year. For what reason I have no idea. Perhaps it's their anniversary. They sit across the table from one another and wait for me. I don't come. They say good-bye and life goes on." Aimee said, grabbing her sweat outfit and putting it on quickly. She knew she was going to have to flee or risk being more abrasive and hurtful than she wanted. This was her one nasty little secret that was to remain buried. Forever.

"Aimee . . ." Lauren said.

"Let it go," Aimee said.

"No."

Aimee stared at her and then made for the door.

"Where are you going?" Lauren said, instantly alarmed.

"Out. I'm going out," Aimee said.

"Aimee . . .wait!" Lauren said.

Lauren stood in the living room staring at the front door. She didn't know whether to run after her or listen to what Aimee was saying. She was indecisive, and then it was too late.

She called Hope.

"Slow down. Tell me what happened from the beginning," Hope counseled.

"Aimee's parents called and they want to meet her and she won't go and she won't tell me why and then she blew out of here and I'm scared."

"Lauren have you ever thought that maybe something went on in Aimee's life that was a little different?"

"What do you mean?"

"Like why she never talks about her parents and why she doesn't want to see them," Hope said.

"I don't know. Maybe they can't accept her being gay or something."

"Has she ever said that?"

"Well, no," Lauren said.

"Then what else?"

"I don't know," Lauren said.

"Do you remember when Aimee had that trouble with Pamela?" Hope queried.

"Which particular episode?" Lauren asked, remembering a seeming mountain of bad moments that Aimee had with Pamela. Lauren knew she had seen but a fraction of what must have gone on. Aimee had told her stories. Lauren had formed the opinion that Aimee and Pamela had had a tumultuous relationship.

Lauren had vowed that she would make a peaceful life for Aimee, but then here she was creating havoc when she'd only wanted to help. She suddenly felt like one of those over-processing lesbians that she and Aimee joked about. But there seemed a thin, lavender line between what was good communication and what was being overly concerned and smothering an issue to death with good intentions. It seemed Lauren had committed her own faux pas.

"The episode when Pamela hurt Aimee," Hope said.

"Yes," Lauren said.

"I think that Aimee might have had the same kind of episode with one of her parents or maybe both," Hope said.

"What makes you think that?" Lauren said.

"It was the way she dealt with Pamela after she hurt her . . ." Hope said, her voice trailing off.

"Yeah, she hit her with a book in retaliation," Lauren said.

"Before that."

"You mean how she tried to hide it and then just went on with her life like it never happened," Lauren said, making the connection and trying to quell the instant anxiety attack she felt creeping around the corner.

"I know this is just supposition on my part, but it might explain her behavior," Hope said, getting a refill.

"That never crossed my mind," Lauren said.

"Abuse is a difficult subject to broach, and if I were you I wouldn't mention it unless Aimee decides to tell you," Hope advised.

"You're right. So I should hold back and let things blow over . . . maybe apologize for trying to be overly helpful."

"Exactly. Let's hope it is something else. Maybe we all guessed wrong," Hope said.

"I hope so. Thank you for counseling me. I'm sorry I'm such a pain in the ass about all this. I get so scared sometimes. I just want to be good for Aimee."

"I know you do, and you are. Don't sell yourself short," Hope said.

"Okay," Lauren said, trying not to sound troubled.

"Just give her time and space."

"I will."

~ ~ ~ ~ ~

Aimee sat at the park watching the ducks waddle around the pond. She was remembering things she thought long buried. She hadn't wanted to be abrupt with Lauren, but she didn't want to tell her either, because then Lauren would see her as a victim. She didn't want to be a victim anymore. When her father made her mother leave, Aimee stopped being a

207

victim in her mind, but telling another person what had gone on reestablished her victim status.

Aimee didn't want to shut Lauren out, but she couldn't figure out any other way to do it. She knew this affected their relationship. She didn't want that. Her only other option was to lie, and she had done too much of that in her life already.

As a child she had pulled her sleeves down when the bruises on her wrists showed. She had played ill during gym class so that she wouldn't have to shower and have others see the bruises on her back. It wasn't until the last beating, the one Aimee couldn't hide, when the lying had to stop. The school nurse was called in, and when everyone looked at what her mother had done, Aimee finally spoke the truth. Her father sent her mother away because he could no longer hide the abuse he knew had gone on. Aimee knew that he had only taken action then because he was being forced to do something. They never spoke of it after that.

What Lauren would never understand is that this showdown happened once a year, and every year Aimee refused to attend. How could she explain to her that Aimee hadn't seen her parents since the crossbow incident and that then it had only been her father, that she had no desire to see either one of them. If her parents could communicate through credit-card bills and the infrequent letter, then why couldn't she do the same? But not to tell Lauren why was to lie. And it was one lie that would affect everything.

Aimee walked around the park surrounded by joggers, dog walkers, and women with their children in strollers. She envied their normal lives. It was getting dark, and she knew she would have to go home soon. But she was still at an impasse. She felt alone and lost. She was angry for having this skeleton clapped around her soul. She craved freedom from the past.

Then she began to understand that maybe saying it aloud would not necessary make her a victim again but would make her stronger for saying the words, for finally confronting her mother with what she had done. Hiding the secret made it bigger and stronger than it had to be. Letting it go might set her free.

Lauren sat by the pool, waiting and trying not to conjure up images of battered children. How could one person be so unfortunate to have only people that hurt her in her life? What sort of a universe, what sort of god, allowed such bad things into this world? Lauren heard the front door close. She sat quiet.

"Hi," Aimee said, shyly. She took off her shoes and slipped her feet in the warm water.

"Are you okay?" Lauren asked.

"Yes, are you?"

Lauren nodded, but didn't look at Aimee.

"I'm sorry," Aimee said.

"Me too. I shouldn't have been pushy," Lauren said, looking at Aimee tentatively.

"You weren't pushy. I was mean and I shouldn't have been," Aimee said, studying her hands. "There are some things I need to explain . . ."

"You don't owe me an explanation," Lauren said.

"But I do. I need to tell you this."

"Okay," Lauren said, meeting Aimee's gaze. She could feel her heart palpitating. What Hope had told her was true.

"The reason I don't want to see my parents is because my mother used to do bad things to me and my father would ignore it. Every year they try to reconcile this fact, and every year I blow them off. I suppose it's my way of punishing them without actually having to say anything."

Lauren nodded. Tears welled up, and she tried to hide them.

"Why are you crying?" Aimee said, pulling Lauren to her.

"I'm sorry," Lauren muttered.

"What are you sorry for? You didn't do anything," Aimee said, wrapping her arms around her.

"I just can't believe someone would hurt you like that," Lauren said.

"It was a long time ago . . . and it's over now, except for one thing. And I need your help," Aimee said.

Lauren pulled away and looked at her. "What do you want me to do?"

"I want you to come to lunch with me."

"Why?"

"Because this time I want to see them."

"Okay," Lauren said, puzzled.

"Thanks for saving the calzones," Aimee said. "I saw them sitting on the stove when I came in."

"I had myself in mind," Lauren responded, glad the evening was resuming its usual course. She hadn't realized until now that she and Aimee led an extremely peaceful life of pleasurable pursuits.

Later when they lay in bed together, Aimee told Lauren the story of her childhood. Lauren felt Aimee's tears as they trickled across Lauren's breast. She suspected that Aimee had never told anyone before. She was glad that they were naked and well loved and in each other's arms when Aimee did want to talk. It seemed only right to be this vulnerable to talk of such things. Lauren knew that Aimee's being able to talk about her childhood was the first step toward healing.

Later, Lauren watched Aimee sleep, her body still wrapped around her own. Aimee's face was filled with peace and calm. Lauren desperately hoped that coming clean and this lunch thing would give Aimee the same kind of peace that sleep brought. She had hoped that after Tuesday Aimee would be free of the guilt and shame she had harbored for so long.

~ ~ ~ ~ ~

Lauren watched Aimee change outfits four times until she settled on a pair of camel-colored pants and a white silk shirt. Lauren dressed in her best power suit, an aquamarine double-breasted blazer with matching pants.

"How do I look?" Aimee asked.

"Beautiful," Lauren replied.

"Are you ready?" Aimee asked.

"Whenever you are," Lauren replied.

When they walked into the Armadillo Café, Aimee's mother and father were having a conversation. Aimee made Lauren stop while she took in the sight. Lauren watched as an older Asian couple sipped their drinks and exchanged anecdotes.

"I bet they haven't talked to each other like that in over ten years," Aimee said.

"Are you okay?" Lauren asked.

"No, I feel sick because this reminds me of the conspiracy they had both perpetrated upon my childhood, the one I'm supposed to keep buried forever because now that I am a grownup it is considered poor taste to bring it up," Aimee replied.

Lauren was doing her best to put a cap on her overactive imagination. She hadn't asked Aimee what exactly they did to her, but Aimee had told her some of the pivotal points. Lauren was left to conjure the rest. Having lunch with people she saw as vicious monsters was almost more than she could bear. But according to Aimee, her presence was absolutely necessary in order to execute her plan.

Lauren did not want to be unsupportive, but this was hardly like taking Aimee to dinner at her parents' house who immediately bonded with the sweet, smart, and witty companion who made their daughter incredibly happy. By the end of dinner Aimee had become an instant family member.

Her mother had pulled Lauren aside in the kitchen and asked her where she had found such a charming woman. Lauren refrained from answering that she'd stolen her from someone else. Instead, she told her she was a friend of Hope and Emerson. Her mother had smiled and told her she had done well.

Aimee's mother and father greeted her enthusiastically, although they did not hug. There were no raised eyebrows at Lauren's presence, even though Aimee had held her hand as they approached the table. Charles Nishimo introduced his wife, Tsuneko, to Lauren and bade them sit down. Lauren could see where Aimee got her looks. Her mother was an extremely attractive woman with no hint of gray in her jet black hair and only very fine wrinkles around her eyes. She was well-dressed, and everything about her breathed culture and poise. Tsuneko was the epitome of charm, and Lauren almost found herself caught in her web of propriety.

"You cut your hair," Tsuneko said, surveying her daughter in a quick summary sort of way like she was checking out her handiwork.

"About five years ago, Mother," Aimee replied. "I cut it all off the night Father bade me to leave off Honour."

"You cut your beautiful hair over a *woman*?" Tsuneko said incredulously.

"Over love, something definitely out of your ken," Aimee replied tersely.

"Let's order," Charles said, flagging a waitress, although Aimee and Lauren had yet to open their menus.

"Let's have one of those," Tsuneko said, pointing to a large, frosty pitcher of margaritas. "And some appetizers."

"Are you feeling festive?" Charles remarked.

"Yes, I am. I haven't seen my darling daughter in five years. I feel most festive," Tsuneko answered.

Lauren watched Aimee cringe.

"It's been longer," Aimee replied.

"And whose fault is that?" Tsuneko said.

"We'll have a pitcher of margaritas and the fried vegetable platter," Charles told the waitress.

"I would say it is your fault," Aimee replied, not distracted in any way from her purpose.

"She was always such an obstinate child, but you see what a driven woman she is now, how well she has done," Tsuneko told Lauren.

"Yes, she is a wonderful woman," Lauren said.

"Is that why you used to beat me all the time as a child?" Aimee asked, her voice even and totally void of emotion. "Is that why we used to move all the time so father could keep the authorities from catching up with you?"

"I don't think this is appropriate lunch conversation," Tsuneko replied.

"Is that why he sent you away when you finally did more damage than he could cover up?"

"This is a family matter, not something to be discussed in front of a stranger," Tsuneko said, looking at Charles for help.

Charles looked passively back at her.

"Lauren knows all about the nasty things you used to do to me."

"How dare you," Tsuneko said, curling her hand around her fork and leaning toward Aimee.

Charles grabbed her hand. "I want you to leave quietly. And this time I don't want you coming back . . . ever. Is that understood? You are to leave Aimee alone, to attempt no further contact."

"If I don't?" Tsuneko countered, glaring at both Aimee and Charles.

"I will revoke all financial compensation and encourage Aimee to take you to court for punitive damages."

"Is this what you want?" Tsuneko asked Aimee.

"I want you out of my life. I want you to know that I hate what you did to me and that I will never forgive you," Aimee replied, staring straight at her mother.

"So be it," Tsuneko replied, standing with a flourish and leaving.

Aimee watched her cross the restaurant and felt the rock that had been cemented to her chest crack into dust. She shook herself clean and smiled at her father.

"I wondered how long it would take you to do that," he said.

"Almost as long as you," Aimee replied, touching her raised glass to his.

Nine

Lauren lay on the bed in a black bra and panties, talking to Emerson on the phone. Aimee was dressing for dinner. She looked at Lauren and felt her face flush when she met her eyes. They'd been together for almost two years, and still Aimee was as hungry now for her as she had been in the those early days of love. It seemed they only got better. She crawled up on the bed behind Lauren, kissing the back of her neck and ears and running her hand up Lauren's smooth inner thigh. Lauren kept talking to Emerson. She smiled at Aimee, who turned her on her back, kissing her stomach and starting to pull her panties off.

"Yes, we're going out to dinner, or at least I thought we were," Lauren said, feeling Aimee's tongue circle her ankle and begin its ascent up her leg. She quivered. She felt Aimee kiss her cunt, teasing, and then deeper.

"Oh my god. I've got to let you go."

"But what about the deal?"

"I can't possibly talk right now," Lauren said, running her hand through Aimee's hair.

"What's she doing to you?" Emerson inquired, hearing Lauren's breath become slightly irregular.

"Something really nice," Lauren said, letting the phone drop.

Hope came in the room to find Emerson smiling and holding the phone, but she wasn't talking.

"What are you doing?"

"Listen," Emerson handed her the phone.

Hope listened. She could hear the soft noises of women making love.

"Emerson, you hang up the phone right now. That's not nice," Hope said.

"I just always wondered what Lauren was like when she made love, and now I kind of know."

"Maybe you could get them to pose for you," Hope chided.

Emerson looked at her brightly. "That's a fucking awesome idea."

"You can't be serious."

"Sure. Lauren always wanted me to do us, but that's not really possible, since the artist is part of the couple, but I could do them. There's not a lot of erotic women stuff out there."

"You'll never talk them into it."

"Bet you fifty bucks I can," Emerson said.

"You're on."

~ ~ ~ ~ ~

"I think doing two women making love would be beautiful. Lord knows it would sell, and I think it would really make a good statement," Lauren said.

"I'm glad you like it. So when can you and Aimee pose for me?"

"What?"

"You heard me. I want to do the two of you."

"Emerson, I am not going to get naked in front of you. I refuse."

"It'll be beautiful, and you'll get to keep the first piece."

"I'm not a model," Lauren replied.

"You should be."

"I can't do it."

"Because I would see you naked?" Emerson said.

"Well, yes. I'm just not comfortable with it. And I don't know how Aimee would feel. What are you doing?"

"Taking off my clothes," Emerson said, pulling her shirt off.

"Why?" Lauren said, feeling herself get panicky.

"So you can see me naked, and then I can see you naked," Emerson said, slipping out of her pants and underwear. It worked every time.

Lauren averted her eyes by looking out the window. Emerson came over and started to unbutton Lauren's blouse.

"What are you doing?"

"Helping you,"

"Emerson," Lauren said, feeling color rise to her face.

"It's for art, Lauren," Emerson said, holding Lauren's hand to stop her from impeding her unbuttoning.

"Oh my god, I can't believe this."

"We're both women. Imagine we just got done playing racquetball and now we're in the locker room."

"I don't play racquetball, and I'm no good at fantasy."

"Work with me, Lauren," Emerson said, undoing her bra and tugging at her pants. "It'll be beautiful, and you know I have to do people I have feelings for or the sculpture doesn't work. Please," Emerson pleaded.

Lauren found it extremely difficult to argue with a naked woman who was rapidly disrobing her. "All right, but I can't guarantee Aimee will go along with it."

"She will," Emerson assured her.

"How do you know?"

"I already asked her," Emerson said, taking a step back and looking at Lauren. "You're beautiful."

"I can't believe you talked me into this," Lauren said, feeling horribly uncomfortable as Emerson walked around her studying her body.

"You have extremely nice breasts," Emerson said.

"Can I get dressed now?"

"I don't suppose you'd let me do a preliminary sketch?"

"Now?"

"Yes."

"No, I'm getting naked for as little time as it takes for you to do this, and you better work fast," Lauren said, trying to get her clothes untangled.

"What do we have here?" Aimee said, trying to sound casual.

Lauren turned bright red. "How do you get me into these things?" she said, quickly putting her shirt on.

"I was talking her into modeling."

"She took off her clothes to get me to take off mine. If I saw her naked then I wouldn't be uncomfortable about being naked in front of her," Lauren babbled. "I know it doesn't make sense, but that's what we were doing . . . honest."

218

Aimee laughed. "All she did was ask me. I should have been more obstinate and gotten the full show."

Emerson whirled around, "See, full show. So when can we start? It's a perfect time for me. I'm waiting on you two."

Aimee felt color coming to her face. She kissed Lauren's neck as she started to get dressed. "Don't do that," Aimee whispered.

"Do what?" Lauren asked.

"Get dressed," Aimee teased.

"So when can we start?"

"Soon," Lauren said, putting her shirt on.

"How about tomorrow? I don't want to be huge for my modeling debut," Aimee said, running her hand over her slightly protruding belly.

Lauren smiled.

"Aren't you going to be the perfect parent," Emerson said. "I'll come by in the morning."

"I can't believe I'm agreeing to this," Lauren said.

"It'll be beautiful. I promise," Emerson said.

Aimee picked up Lauren's pants and locked the door.

"Hey, where are you going with those," Lauren said, coming toward her.

"I thought we should practice," Aimee said, pushing her toward the bedroom.

Lauren smiled.

Pamela took Lindy's hand and went into the living room. "Want a drink?"

"Please," Lindy said, smiling and refraining from saying that what she really wanted was Pamela. But Dr. Severson was worth waiting for. It had taken her this long, and now she was past being determined. Lindy was quickly wandering into the land of being thoroughly obsessed.

Lindy studied the large bronze figures in the living room. "What are these? They're beautiful," she said, running her hand along the sculptures. One was a woman standing, and the other was of two women making love.

Pamela stood looking at them. "I bought them at a gallery downtown."

"I like them. Anyone you know?" Lindy teased.

Pamela turned toward the kitchen to get drinks, "No, I just like the content."

"Yes, they're nice."

"They are nice, but not as nice as you," Pamela said, putting their drinks on the bar and unbuttoning Lindy's blouse.

DEATH BY DEATH by Claire McNab. 167 pp. 5th Denise
Cleever Thriller.   ISBN 1-931513-34-1 $12.95

CAUGHT IN THE NET by Jessica Thomas. 188 pp. A Wickedly
observant story of mystery, danger and love in Provincetown.
                                     ISBN 1-931513-54-6 $12.95

DREAMS FOUND by Lyn Denison. 201 pp. Australian Riley embarks
on a journey to meet her birth mother . . . and gains not just a family, but
the love of her life.   ISBN 1-931513-58-9 $12.95

A MOMENT'S INDISCRETION by Peggy J. Herring.
Jackie is torn between her better judgment and the overwhelming attraction she feels for Valerie.   ISBN# 1-931513-59-7 $12.95

IN EVERY PORT by Karin Kallmaker. 224 pp. Jessica's sexy,
adventuresome travels.   ISBN 1-931513-36-8 $12.95

TOUCHWOOD by Karin Kallmaker. 240 pp. Loving
May/December romance.   ISBN 1-931513-37-6 $12.95

WATERMARK by Karin Kallmaker. 248 pp. One burning
question . . . how to lead her back to love? ISBN 1-931513-38-4 $12.95

EMBRACE IN MOTION by Karin Kallmaker. 240 pp. A
whirlwind love affair.   ISBN 1-931513-39-2 $12.95

ONE DEGREE OF SEPARATION by Karin Kallmaker. 232 pp.
Can an Iowa City librarian find love and passion when a California
girl surfs into the close-knit Dyke Capital of the Midwest?

                                     ISBN 1-931513-30-9 $12.95

CRY HAVOC A Detective Franco Mystery by Baxter Clare. 240 pp. A dead hustler with a headless rooster in his lap sends Lt. L.A. Franco headfirst against Mother Love.   ISBN 1-931513931-7 $12.95

DISTANT THUNDER by Peggy J. Herring. 294 pp. Bankrobbing drifter Cordy awakens strange new feelings in Leo in this romantic tale set in the old West.   ISBN 1-931513-28-7 $12.95

COP OUT by Claire McNab. 216 pp. 4th Detective Inspector Carol Ashton Mystery.   ISBN 1-931513-29-5 $12.95

BLOOD LINK by Claire McNab. 159 pp. 15th Detective Inspector Carol Ashton Mystery. Is Carol unwittingly playing into a deadly plan?   ISBN 1-931513-27-9 $12.95

TALK OF THE TOWN by Saxon Bennett. 239 pp. With enough beer, barbecue and B.S., anything is possible!   ISBN 1-931513-18-X $12.95

MAYBE NEXT TIME by Karin Kallmaker. 256 pp. Sabrina Starling has it all: fame, money, women—and pain. Nothing hurts like the one that got away.   ISBN 1-931513-26-0 $12.95

WHEN GOOD GIRLS GO BAD: A Motor City Thriller by Therese Szymanski. 230 pp. Brett, Randi, and Allie join forces to stop a serial killer.   ISBN 1-931513-11-2   12.95

A DAY TOO LONG: A Helen Black Mystery by Pat Welch. 328 pp. This time Helen's fate is in her own hands.   ISBN 1-931513-22-8 $12.95

THE RED LINE OF YARMALD by Diana Rivers. 256 pp. The Hadra's only hope lies in a magical red line . . . Climactic sequel to *Clouds of War.*   ISBN 1-931513-23-6 $12.95

OUTSIDE THE FLOCK by Jackie Calhoun. 224 pp. Jo embraces her new love and life.   ISBN 1-931513-13-9 $12.95

LEGACY OF LOVE by Marianne K. Martin. 224 pp. Read the whole Sage Bristo story.   ISBN 1-931513-15-5 $12.95

STREET RULES: A Detective Franco Mystery by Baxter Clare. 304 pp. Gritty, fast-paced mystery with compelling Detective L.A. Franco   ISBN 1-931513-14-7 $12.95

RECOGNITION FACTOR: 4th Denise Cleever Thriller by Claire McNab. 176 pp. Denise Cleever tracks a notorious terrorist to America.　　　　　　　ISBN 1-931513-24-4　$12.95

NORA AND LIZ by Nancy Garden. 296 pp. Lesbian romance by the author of *Annie on My Mind*.　ISBN 1931513-20-1　$12.95

MIDAS TOUCH by Frankie J. Jones. 208 pp. Sandra had everything but love.　　　　　　ISBN 1-931513-21-X　$12.95

BEYOND ALL REASON by Peggy J. Herring. 240 pp. A romance hotter than Texas.　　　　ISBN 1-9513-25-2　$12.95

ACCIDENTAL MURDER: 14th Detective Inspector Carol Ashton Mystery by Claire McNab. 208 pp.Carol Ashton tracks an elusive killer.　　　　　ISBN 1-931513-16-3　$12.95

SEEDS OF FIRE:Tunnel of Light Trilogy, Book 2 by Karin Kallmaker writing as Laura Adams. 274 pp. Intriguing sequel to *Sleight of Hand*.　　　　　　ISBN 1-931513-19-8　$12.95

DRIFTING AT THE BOTTOM OF THE WORLD by Auden Bailey. 288 pp. Beautifully written first novel set in Antarctica.　　　　　　　　ISBN 1-931513-17-1　$12.95

CLOUDS OF WAR by Diana Rivers. 288 pp. Women unite to defend Zelindar!　　　　　ISBN 1-931513-12-0　$12.95

DEATHS OF JOCASTA: 2nd Micky Knight Mystery by J.M. Redmann. 408 pp. Sexy and intriguing Lambda Literary Award-nominated mystery.　　　　ISBN 1-931513-10-4　$12.95

LOVE IN THE BALANCE by Marianne K. Martin. 256 pp. The classic lesbian love story, back in print! ISBN 1-931513-08-2 $12.95

THE COMFORT OF STRANGERS by Peggy J. Herring. 272 pp. Lela's work was her passion . . . until now. ISBN 1-931513-09-0　$12.95

CHICKEN by Paula Martinac. 208 pp. Lynn finds that the only thing harder than being in a lesbian relationship is ending one.　　　　　　　　　ISBN 1-931513-07-4　$11.95

TAMARACK CREEK by Jackie Calhoun. 208 pp. An intriguing story of love and danger.　　　ISBN 1-931513-06-6　$11.95

DEATH BY THE RIVERSIDE: 1st Micky Knight Mystery by
J.M. Redmann. 320 pp. Finally back in print, the book that
launched the Lambda Literary Award-winning Micky Knight
mystery series.   ISBN 1-931513-05-8 $11.95

EIGHTH DAY: A Cassidy James Mystery by Kate Calloway.
272 pp. In the eighth installment of the Cassidy James
mystery series, Cassidy goes undercover at a camp for troubled
teens.   ISBN 1-931513-04-X $11.95

MIRRORS by Marianne K. Martin. 208 pp. Jean Carson and Shayna
Bradley fight for a future together.   ISBN 1-931513-02-3 $11.95

THE ULTIMATE EXIT STRATEGY: A Virginia Kelly
Mystery by Nikki Baker. 240 pp. The long-awaited return of
the wickedly observant Virginia Kelly.   ISBN 1-931513-03-1 $11.95

FOREVER AND THE NIGHT by Laura DeHart Young. 224 pp.
Desire and passion ignite the frozen Arctic in this exciting
sequel to the classic romantic adventure *Love on the Line*.
                                   ISBN 0-931513-00-7 $11.95

WINGED ISIS by Jean Stewart. 240 pp. The long-awaited
sequel to *Warriors of Isis* and the fourth in the exciting Isis
series.   ISBN 1-931513-01-5 $11.95

ROOM FOR LOVE by Frankie J. Jones. 192 pp. Jo and Beth
must overcome the past in order to have a future together.
                                   ISBN 0-9677753-9-6 $11.95

THE QUESTION OF SABOTAGE by Bonnie J. Morris.
144 pp. A charming, sexy tale of romance, intrigue, and
coming of age.   ISBN 0-9677753-8-8 $11.95

SLEIGHT OF HAND by Karin Kallmaker writing as
Laura Adams. 256 pp. A journey of passion, heartbreak
and triumph that reunites two women for a final chance at
their destiny.   ISBN 0-9677753-7-X $11.95

MOVING TARGETS: A Helen Black Mystery by Pat Welch.
240 pp. Helen must decide if getting to the bottom of a mystery
is worth hitting bottom.   ISBN 0-9677753-6-1 $11.95

CALM BEFORE THE STORM by Peggy J. Herring. 208 pp. Colonel Robicheaux retires from the military and comes out of the closet. ISBN 0-9677753-1-0 $12.95

OFF SEASON by Jackie Calhoun. 208 pp. Pam threatens Jenny and Rita's fledgling relationship. ISBN 0-9677753-0-2 $11.95

WHEN EVIL CHANGES FACE: A Motor City Thriller by Therese Szymanski. 240 pp. Brett Higgins is back in another heart-pounding thriller. ISBN 0-9677753-3-7 $11.95

BOLD COAST LOVE by Diana Tremain Braund. 208 pp. Jackie Claymont fights for her reputation and the right to love the woman she chooses. ISBN 0-9677753-2-9 $11.95

THE WILD ONE by Lyn Denison. 176 pp. Rachel never expected that Quinn's wild yearnings would change her life forever. ISBN 0-9677753-4-5 $12.95

SWEET FIRE by Saxon Bennett. 224 pp. Welcome to Heroy—the town with the most lesbians per capita than any other place on the planet! ISBN 0-9677753-5-3 $11.95

Visit

Bella Books

at

BellaBooks.com

or call our toll-free number

1-800-729-4992